GLORIA DON'T SPEAK

"Lucy Apps is one of the most exciting new voices in fiction. In *Gloria Don't Speak*, she crafts a profound, beautifully observed portrait of loneliness, loyalty and one woman's search for community. Tender, nuanced and full of heart, it will stay with me for a very long time."
Kia Abdullah, *Next of Kin* and *Those People Next Door*

"Lucid and beautifully observed, this story of a vulnerable person navigating the world brims with pinpoint detail and creeping threat. A brilliant and assured debut."
Simon Wroe, *Chop, Chop* and *Ghost Month*

GLORIA DON'T SPEAK

Lucy Apps

WEATHERGLASS BOOKS

GLORIA DON'T SPEAK

For Benjamin Zephaniah

1999

1

Jack is talking about the end of the world. Gloria listens. He's on about everything breaking down and burning. His words slide over each other in her head.

She concentrates on the circle of ketchup she's squeezing onto her paper and the way the room smells of vinegar, and the oil that sits on the skin of the chips and shines her fingertips smooth. Jack's house. Jack smiles at her and raises his can then sips from it and nods. Gloria looks down at the light gleaming on the red circle of ketchup. It's Monday afternoon in July. It's summer and she's finished college and they haven't had Christmas yet.

Jack eats his chips like he's angry with the air in front of him. He picks up his can and takes swigs and puts it down again. He keeps on doing the same motion. He don't just hold it in his hand. Gloria copies him with her Coke,

picking it up and drinking then putting it down, her fingers all cold and wet from the tin.

'Want a beer?' Jack says.

Gloria don't speak.

'You can't be a kid all your life,' Jack says.

Wanna beer wanna beer wanna beer.

She plays Jack's words over in her head, finding the rhythm. She rocks a little in time to the sound. Inside her mouth she runs her tongue over her teeth. She can feel her tongue on the inside of her cheeks and the hard dips and jags of her molars. Her teeth are warm from chips and sweet from ketchup. She don't want a beer. Jack has handed her his drink before and told her to take a sip. It was bitter and like metal. Not sweet.

Jack watches her rock for a moment. When she don't answer, he says, 'Suit yourself.'

Mum won't like Jack. Gloria already knows, she can guess. If Mum finds out about Jack she won't let Gloria see him no more. And Gloria don't want to stop seeing him. She walks the pavements by herself all day long in the heat, in her pedal pushers and Adidas trainers that are too small for her now, but she still likes them. She walks up and down and she remembers summer days when she used to go on playschemes and they used to take her cinema and swimming but those days are finished now. Now college is over, it's all finished, she walks around. She goes to the park and she finds a bench to sit. If people start bothering her too much then she gets up and goes away to another park. Another bench. All the boys playing football are so loud and they shout all the time, and they come to sit on the bench and they look at her and frown and squint their eyes at her, kiss their teeth and say, 'Move, man.' So rude.

There's one time when they tell her to move and she gets angry, because she's there first sitting on the bench, so why should she have to move? She says, 'No.'

And one of the boys says, 'Move you dumb bitch, get out of our way, this is our bench ya heard. Fuck off.' And they all look at her, their eyes really hard and cold like they want to hit her, their hoods pulled up even though it's hot. Gloria hates them boys then. She gets fed up. Finding another bench and then another bench. And she gets bored by herself all day. She don't like walking around and around on her own. Jack makes things different. Even the same places, they seem new.

Gloria keeps on eating her chips. Hot vinegary potato mushing in her cheeks and sweet sharp ketchup on her tongue. Jack is quiet for a bit, then he starts up again.

'Five months. Five months and this country's going down.' He shakes his head and laughs. 'Going under. Whole fucking show's over. Can't cope with the calendar. It'll be havoc. Chaos. They won't know what to do.' He laughs again. He picks up his can and drinks a bit more. 'It's not long left,' he says. He taps his fingers on the arm of his chair.

Jack looks a bit like Westlife. Gloria don't like them but she knows what they look like. His hair is shorter but his face is pretty, and he looks nice. His blue eyes glint at her over his can when he asks if she wants a beer. When he wears a vest she can see all the muscles moving in his arms. Gloria don't speak a lot and Jack don't mind. Other people always say Gloria you're too quiet, or What do you think Gloria? Which one would you like? Jack knows she'll have what he has, and they like the same things mostly, so it don't matter.

'I'll be out on me own, gonna hole up somewhere just outside the city,' Jack says. 'It's gonna be mental, you know that. Planes'll fall from the sky and that. You know what I'm gonna do? I'll stay around for a bit, take what I can, you know, stock up. Then I'll find somewhere just outside London, probably Essex probably, it's closest. Or Kent. Somewhere by a river, near some water. Somewhere small, where I can see all the exits and entrances. So I can keep an eye. I'll have my padlock, that's one thing I need to take. A decent rucksack. I'll take me knife but I'll get hold of a gun. I'll stay there by the river, somewhere small. It's all I need. I can make a fire out of flint. Just dry bits of wood and that. I'll go into the city on raids. Take food. Cans and that. I don't need much. Come with me if you like. I'll look after you. You'll have to be tough though. It won't be easy. Do you know how to build a fire?'

He looks at Gloria.

'Have you ever slept outdoors?' he says. 'You got a lot to learn. It's not easy getting sleep in the cold on hard ground. You gotta keep your feet dry. You've had it too soft. You need to stick with me Gloria, when the shit hits the fan.'

Jack stares ahead for a bit, imagining how it's gonna be.

Then he laughs and shrugs. He takes a sip from his can. He scoops up a handful of chips and chews hard.

The first time Gloria meets Jack, she's walking home from college. It's the first warm day in the year. The sun is shining. The weather is so nice Mrs Uddin lets them do maths outdoors, on the grass. Gloria's class is special needs so they do lessons different from the other kids. For maths they sit round in a circle, counting up cardboard coins and learning how much to pay for things in shops.

Gloria is too hot walking home. Her coat feels big and bulky. She takes it off and holds it, but it keeps slipping down out of her hands and dragging on the ground. Her feet get caught on the sleeves and trip her up. She hates this coat. Hates carrying it. She wants to throw it in the bin, or drop it and leave it behind, but she can't because Mum will be mad.

The air is all soft, stirring with the sounds of traffic and people talking and shouting. Down the end of the road where the crossing is, a man is sitting on a bench. He's smoking. He's watching the people walk by and all the cars going past in front of him, the sunlight shining off their windows. Across the way a group of kids from Gloria's college cluster outside the chicken shop, shouting and laughing. Gloria don't have money on her for the chicken shop but she ain't hungry anyway. She just wants to stop outdoors where it's nice and busy, and watch things happen and be a part of it.

Gloria sits down on the bench with the man. She sits the other end of the bench from him. He keeps on smoking, looking ahead. Then he turns and looks at her. He looks at her for a while. She don't look back at him. She looks away, over the road at the sun shining on the bricks of the pub opposite, turning them a soft golden colour.

'All these pubs are gonna close down soon,' the man says. 'It's all changing round here.'

Gloria looks at him then. He's still watching her.

'You won't know this place,' he says. 'Thirty years ago to today.' He laughs a little bit and keeps on smoking. 'Some bloke just come asking me for money,' he says. He shakes his head. 'Can you believe it? I ain't got no money and they come here asking me for money.'

Gloria knows what he is talking about. This happens to her a lot too.

'Sometimes this place does me head in,' the man says. 'You get me?'

Gloria looks away again, back at the traffic and the group of kids from her college eating their fried chicken over the other side of the road. They are all laughing at something, their mouths open and happy.

'You don't talk much,' the man says. But he don't say it like a lot of people do, like they are telling her off and saying she should talk. He's just saying.

'Jack,' he says. He puts his hand out for Gloria to shake. His eyes are a sharp blue and the sunlight shines in them, the way it shines in everything on the street.

Gloria shakes his hand. His skin is warm and dry.

'What's your name?' he says.

'Gloria,' she says.

'Gloria. That's a nice name,' he says.

She don't say nothing after that and neither does he. They both sit there for a bit longer at either end of the bench, watching the day soft and warm around them. Then Gloria remembers that Mum will be getting home from work soon, and if Gloria ain't in from college by the time Mum gets back, then Mum will be worried and she'll cuss her. So Gloria gets up and leaves Jack sitting on the bench. He puts his hand up when she leaves, like the beginning of a wave, but he don't move it from side to side. He just holds his hand up and nods. She walks away from him and crosses the road.

After that Gloria sees him there on the bench a lot. He always says hello to her and nods at her. If the weather's nice she sits down for a little while and he talks to her. He talks about different things. He don't mind if she talks back or not.

One day he says, 'I'm going for a walk, just over the park. Fancy coming?'

Gloria nods. She gets up and goes with him. They walk around the park together, watching the little kids on the swings and the climbing frames, and all the kids from Gloria's college over by the metal benches, eating chips and shouting at each other and blazing weed.

'Cor they're a noisy lot ain't they,' Jack says, 'I ain't surprised you don't bother with them. Can't see you pissing about like that.'

He smiles at Gloria and blows out smoke from his

cigarette. And she thinks it's better being with him and walking around than being over there with them kids talking and laughing. Jack talks about lots of things Gloria's never heard of, or if she has heard of them she ain't really interested, so she don't pay enough attention to make it all stick together in her head. But it don't matter. Jack just chats to her and he don't care if she talks back or not, so she just needs to like listening. And she does like it. Listening and walking, his voice playing rhythms in her ear. He buys her drinks from the shop. He smokes cigarettes. Gloria never smokes because it's bad for you, but still the smell of his smoke mixed with the sunny smell of the day gets her just right. The mud and the grass and the tarmac and the traffic fumes.

Jack talks about the end of the world a lot. He keeps counting, watching the calendar, telling Gloria how long it is until the Millennium, when everything will fall apart and he can run away and find his place. He talks and talks about how it's gonna be. He is waiting the summer out, waiting the city out, counting down to zero. Gloria listens.

'When something's ready to break it breaks,' he says. 'You can't always wait till the right time. You can't always wait for everything else to break with you. Sometimes you reach too much. You're ready to snap. Sometimes everything else ain't at breaking point but you are.'

He looks at her.

'You know what I mean Gloria?' he says. 'Year zero.'

'Yeah,' Gloria says, and he smiles.

'You ain't got a clue. Not a fucking clue. I'm going for a fag.'

He rolls a fag and goes over to the window to smoke it, and Gloria is sitting there, waiting for him to break. He blows smoke out into the street. His street is all houses, no shops. Across the way from his place is a little patch of grass, not a park, just an open place. The grass is all brown and dry now in the sun. Over the other side of it you can see more houses, and Canary Wharf behind them, silver-grey against the sky. Jack says he don't want the flat to smell of smoke but it still does. He has one small room with a folding canvas chair and an old armchair and a folding table that falls down sometimes. There are letters and leaflets on the table. There is a small TV. There is a sink and a microwave. The bed is in the corner. The duvet is always hanging off it, drooping like he's just thrown it back and got up a little while ago.

Gloria is not at breaking point. She likes summer. She likes being outside in the sunshine. Sometimes she gets worried when she thinks about college being finished for good now, and what will happen next? But mostly it's okay. She don't understand. He's right.

'You don't see it, Gloria,' Jack says. 'You don't see the things going wrong, the way things are. But I do.'

*

Mum says, 'You need to get used to amusing yourself, Gloria. You're an adult now, no one's gonna entertain you. I've gotta go work. I've gotta be able to trust you.'

So Gloria makes sure that when Mum gets in from work she is at home, sitting on the sofa watching TV. That's the agreement. Not the TV part, just that Gloria has to be home before Mum gets in from work. She don't have to watch TV, she just chooses to do that.

'I'm trusting you, Gloria,' Mum says. 'You're a grown-up now. I can't keep you locked away forever. So just make sure you're indoors time I get home from work. Don't go giving me a moment's worry. Promise me.'

When Mum comes home she calls out 'Gloria?' and sticks her head round the door and sees Gloria sitting on the sofa. She sighs a little bit, and smiles like she's completed a difficult job. Then she goes through into the kitchen.

'Want tea?' she says. When Gloria don't answer she accepts it as a no. She comes back with her mug after a bit and sits down next to Gloria on the sofa. She ducks forward and sniffs at Gloria's hair.

'You smell of fags,' she says. She takes Gloria's chin and turns Gloria's face towards her.

Gloria looks away.

'Who you been hanging around with, Gloria? Who's been smoking around you?'

'In the park,' Gloria says.

'People smoking in the park was they?'

Gloria don't speak.

Mum is still holding Gloria's chin. She is looking at Gloria and frowning. Gloria pulls away and sits back, staring at the TV.

'You met anyone?' Mum says. 'Any new friends?'

Gloria shakes her head.

'Sure? You ain't been hanging around with someone who smokes? No one you want to tell me about?'

But Gloria can tell she is not expecting an answer.

2

When she's had enough of walking by herself and the sun is making her head sweat or the boys are getting too rude, Gloria goes round Jack's. Sometimes he's got work. And those days she gets a heavy feeling inside her, because she has to go back to walking around the parks and the streets on her own and trying not to attract too much attention. She knows where Jasvinder lives but she don't know if she's allowed to just go round there and ring on the doorbell. And Jasvinder's mum don't let Jasvinder out, so the two of them would have to sit inside anyway. Gloria don't really want to sit indoors, but if she's going to then she'll do it at Jack's, not all by herself at home. And not at Jasvinder's, with Jasvinder's mum watching them and keep trying to talk to her. But when she goes to see Jack she always feels a little bit frightened too, like she don't know what's going to happen next.

When she gets to his, Jack buzzes her in through the front door, and Gloria climbs the stairs and knocks on Jack's door, and Jack opens it and says, 'Alright Gloria, let's go out yeah. I can't take being shut up indoors no more.'

Gloria's pleased. She likes it when they go out. Jack don't normally like to go outside. He likes it he says, but not the people. Gloria don't like some of the people, some of them are alright, and she is one too, but she don't argue with him. There's no point, and she wants him to keep letting her come in his place.

Jack sticks a cigarette in his mouth and zips his jacket up even though it's too hot for a jacket. They go onto the Greenway and walk and walk. The footpath snakes along the backs of houses and past railway lines. There are no cars along here, only people, on bikes and on foot, jogging or walking dogs. Blackberries grow in the hedgerow. The blunt smell of sewage spews up through the concrete vents in the ground.

Jack don't say much. He unzips his jacket but he keeps it on. He is frowning all the time because of the sun in his eyes. Gloria watches the sunlight bright on the bushes, softening the backs of houses, and flashing and gleaming on the trains going past. There are people on the grass with bin bags, using sticks to pick up all the litter. Jack raises his hand to them and does a thumbs up. 'Nice to see someone doing something fucking decent for a change,' he shouts. He's walking too fast for Gloria. He keeps shaking his head over and over, quick and angry. She can't keep up. She falls behind. After a bit he slows down and walks beside her.

They walk all the way down to Jenkins Tip. Gloria can't do that on her own cos Mum says it's not safe. Ignore me if you want Gloria, you wanna see yourself get raped and mugged girl, don't come crying to me. But Gloria is with Jack now. It don't matter that some people might want to rape and mug her, it don't matter that all the kids in her college blaze without her, it don't matter that she sits in the park by herself and all the boys tell her to fuck off from their bench. When Jack's there no one will hurt her then.

'Had a rough day yesterday,' he says, beside her. 'This cunt's telling me what to do, do this do that, bossing me around like he's better than me. I accept he's the boss yeah, but he don't need to talk to me like that. Fucking talking down to me. There's no need for it. What's wrong with treating people with a bit of respect?'

Jack looks at Gloria. She looks back at him. He takes a drag on his cigarette. He's walking with his shoulders rolling, the energy and anger bouncing through them.

'I should of punched the geezer,' he says. 'Knocked him out sparko. I'm too nice. I should of showed him. I done it before, my last job. Some cunt started on me so I dropped him. Boom, one punch. Put him on his arse. That's the way you gotta do it. Show people you can't be messed with. Otherwise every cunt messes with you. I tell ya, if this fella starts on me again I'm gonna fucking… I ain't gonna take it.' He shakes his head, a lot of times. 'Fucking people do my fucking head in,' he says.

Back at his place, he puts the telly on. It's kids' TV. The *Art Attack* man is building a big picture out of black bin liners and plastic bottles. Jack sits and watches for a bit, leaning back in his chair, his head to one side. 'How you think he does that?' he says. 'He got it drawn out in chalk like or what?'

Korwhat. Likorwhat.

Gloria watches the man lay bottles out one after the other, fast, like he don't have to stop and think about it. Like he knows it's going to turn out good.

Jack watches, tapping his foot, biting his nail. His leg is twitching. 'It's a con,' he says. 'Massive fucking con, like he ain't just doing that. It's all set up for show.' He looks at Gloria quick then looks away. He shakes his head.

'It's a fucking joke,' he says. 'Anyone can do that if it's all drawn out for them, know what I mean?'

Gloria don't speak. She can tell Jack's angry. She presses her tongue onto her teeth, making her tongue hurt.

'You don't get what I'm on about at all, do you?' he says.

He's looking at her properly now. She goes still. Jack's eyes are so blue, it's a strange colour in a human face. Some people's eyes are blue like stone or blue like water. But Jack's eyes are blue like plastic. They look like they are made of tinted plastic stuck on over the white.

'Let me tell you what it means,' Jack says. 'You finished school now ain't you? Ain't you?'

Suddenly he is expecting an answer from her. He looks at her, waiting. Gloria nods.

'Know what comes next?' he says. 'What's happening to you next? Has anyone told you?'

She waits.

'Has anyone told you?' he says again.

Then he droops a bit.

'You'll have something,' he says. 'Someone like you, you'll have something. Your mum'll fight for you. There'll be funding or some special school or college. Social workers. You'll be alright. You don't need to know, do you. Me' – he leans forward – 'I got no one. Nothing. No one tells me what comes next. I have to make it up meself. Out of nothing. This is it, this fucking place. All I got.'

He's staring at her.

'Do you get it? Sometimes I get scared, Gloria. So what happens when I get scared? What do I do? I just have to pick meself up don't I? Who gives a shit how I'm feeling? You never say a fucking word.'

Don't get wha'm onabout don't get wha'm onabout.

Gloria puts his words through her head in a cycle, trying to make something soothing from them, something with a rhythm. She don't like it when he talks on and on like this.

'You're just a pretty face and big tits,' Jack says. 'Not that I'm complaining. Not that there's anything wrong with that.'

He smiles at her. 'Smile Gloria,' he says. 'I'm giving you a compliment darling. I'm saying you look nice.'

He stands up. He breaks across the space between them. He reaches out and touches her, puts a hand on her cheek then down onto her shoulder. His finger strokes her neck.

Tickles. She bends her head over, curves her neck away.

'You don't even know what you got,' he says.

Wrongwi that wrongwi that wrongwi that.

Gloria's heart pounds. Her throat is drying closed. She wants him to touch her the whole time he never touched her. She looks at his hands and thinks how warm his fingers would be on her. But now it don't feel warm or special. It just feels normal and boring. Like anyone poking against her neck with ordinary fingers and skin. Touching her too much. And he's too close. Looking at her too much. 'Stop,' she says.

'What you mean stop?' he says. 'I'm only touching your neck. You're in my house and you wanna tell me I can't reach out and touch you, like mates? We're mates ain't we?'

He keeps his hand on her neck. He wraps his fingers round the back, his thumb round the front. He strokes his thumb up and down over her throat.

'I can touch you,' Jack says. 'I can do what I like.'

Gloria swallows. She feels her neck pushing out against his thumb. He keeps stroking his thumb up and down.

'All them months we been talking, all them months you been coming to my flat, and I never done nothing. Been buying you food and I never done nothing. And you wanna act like you can't trust me?'

He presses his thumb right into her skin. He squeezes his fingers tight so his hand is tight on her throat. He squeezes a bit more. Just for a moment. She can feel that if he presses harder she won't be able to breathe.

'Stay still,' he says. 'Show me you trust me.'

'Jack,' she says. His thumb pushes in and out against her throat as she speaks.

'Shh. Stay still. Don't cry. Just stay still. I'm gonna count to five. In my head. Stay still. Don't move. I'm keeping my hand here. Feel how tight I'm keeping my hand? Just tight enough. I'm not gonna choke you. So just trust me. You have to just keep still and show me you can trust me while I count.'

Gloria's neck is pounding against his hand.

'Quiet,' he says.

She don't make a noise.

This is everything changed now, between them. She thought it was her and him being friends and they both like eating chips and he likes talking and she likes listening, trussmetrussmetrussme, and he has no one to talk to and she has no one to listen to, so they can fit with each other. And he looks nice. But now his face looks hard, all plastic, not just his eyes. Gloria can feel the tears starting in her eyes and nose. She's too frightened to cry properly. She don't know what he will do if she makes a noise. She don't know what he will do now at all. So she lets the tears run onto her cheeks and she don't move to wipe them away and she don't cry. She remembers Mum saying, When you're a grown up you're gonna have to learn to cry without making a noise, it's no good bawling like a baby all your life Gloria. This is the first time she's ever done it. To cry without making a noise. Maybe she's a grown-up.

3

When Mum gets home that evening she says, 'Make me a cuppa tea will you Glor, I'm parched.'

Gloria is sitting frozen on the sofa. Outside the day is bright even though it's late. The sunshine comes through the net curtain, making it glow white so Gloria can't see the street through it.

'Ain't you gonna make me a cuppa tea?' Mum says.

Gloria shakes her head. Even though he ain't there, she can still feel Jack's hand on her throat. It makes her stay really still like he told her to.

'Bloody ungrateful,' Mum says. She goes into the kitchen and puts the kettle on. Gloria can hear it bubbling. In the kitchen, Mum starts playing Tracy Chapman and singing along. 'You get up on the wrong side of bed today or what?' she calls.

Gloria hears the chink chink chink of spoon on mug, stirring. She don't move. She keeps her neck tight and stiff, Jack's hand still there.

Mum comes back in, holding her tea. The music keeps happening in the kitchen.

'What you gonna do with yourself Gloria?' Mum says.

She blows on her tea, looking at Gloria.

'What you gonna do when summer's over and you can't walk around outside no more, eh? We'll have to find something for you to do.'

Mum sits down on the armchair.

'There'll be something,' she says. 'There'll be something.' She closes her eyes and tilts her head back. She's talking really quiet like she's not even talking to Gloria at all.

Funding or some special school or college. Social workers. Gloria feels something pressing against her. Pushing her further against the sofa so she can't get up and go nowhere. She stays still but really she wants to run. It feels like she'll be stuck this way forever and she don't know a way out until she dies. And when you die you just stop being there and the world keeps happening without you. She can see herself put in a coffin and put in a hole in the ground and Mum crying and then years later new people living in this house and sleeping in her room and they don't even know she was ever here. It all just keeps happening and keeps happening. She could spend every day for the rest of her life staying still on this sofa afraid to move and it don't matter. Don't make no difference. There's noise. She's making noise like Mum always tells her not to. Stop yelling, you're too old for all this. Even though Jack showed her earlier how to cry quietly. But she can't do it twice in one day, it's a lot.

'Gloria,' Mum says, 'what's wrong? Come here darling. Shush, shush now.'

Mum gets up and moves to sits beside Gloria. She puts her arms around Gloria and Gloria hugs her hard. Gloria pushes her face into Mum's shoulder, between her shoulder and her neck, and she tries to be all wrapped up. She makes more noise. It feels nice. Sobbing and sobbing then gasping for breath. Shush shush now. It makes the pictures of Jack go away.

'You need to tell me what's got you so worked up, Gloria. Has something happened?'

Gloria pulls away. She pushes her face into the back of the sofa and down, so her face is pressed between the seat and the back, where the cushions make a corner. No light. She opens her eyes. All dark. She shouts in the dark.

What's gotyaso worktup.

She reaches out and grabs Mum's arm and pulls it close so she can smell Mum's skin. She thinks about biting Mum's arm. Her teeth in the soft warm skin, a tight mouthful, her tongue and jaw full. Digging her nails in and feeling Mum's skin split and hurt. Wet blood. Gloria strokes at her mum's arm instead. She bites her teeth into her own warm tongue, the soft and the hard together in her mouth.

Mum hits her bum. 'Gloria you're nineteen! I don't care if you're special needs, you're too old to be burying your face in the sofa with your arse in the air. You need to sit up and open your mouth and tell me what's the problem. What's happened? Has someone touched you?'

Open yourmouth open yourmouth.

Gloria opens her mouth wide and pushes her tongue against the cushion. Her tongue and lips scrape against the fabric. Soft. Soft dark world holding her. Salt smell of spit like hot ocean. She wants to be really stuck, pushed in on all sides so it's like an adventure in the sticky darkness, pressing on her sides and the top of her head and face. She flexes her head up and down so she can feel how Jack's hand ain't there no more, just sofa cushion cover, raw against her skin. She lifts her face and sees all the light dazzling her. The sudden fresh air. Smash back down again into the sofa all wet from spit and tears. She screams. Up and down again, hitting her head on the cushions, scraping on her face then air on her face then scraping on her face. She screams and cries. She keeps hitting her head up and down.

4

After he puts his hand round her neck, Gloria don't go back to Jack's. She walks around by herself. It rains for two days. She stays indoors and watches TV. She cooks noodles for herself by breaking them into a mug and boiling the kettle and pouring the water on them. Her favourite mug is a green-blue colour, like the colour the sea is in pictures. The sea is not that colour in real life, it's grey and brown when you go to Southend. And the mug is round and fat and wide and it's thick, so you can hold it tight and it don't burn your hands. Gloria always uses that mug. When her fork taps the bottom it makes a soft chime.

When the weather clears up and it's hot she goes outside and walks around again. Children play in the streets, playing football in the road. Groups of kids hang around in the parks. Kids play cricket in the market on the days when there's no stalls.

Gloria walks up to Wanstead Flats. Wanstead Flats is a big open grass area, like fields. You can see a long way. It's not close to Jack's house and there's a lot of space and a pond and it's peaceful. And there's woods. Gloria likes it there in the sunshine, the long walk all the way up Green Street to get there, and then the sunlight shining on the water and through the trees. There are a lot of dogs and there are children riding bikes.

Green Street is always busy. Gloria goes up and down there a lot. There's lots of colour, racks of shoes and fabrics glittering in the sun, sequins catching the light. There are boxes of mangoes and sacks of rice stacked on the pavement. In the market men shout about fruit and vegetables for a pound. The air smells sour, of hot rubbish. People sit on benches eating corn and samosas. Kids have set the bin on the corner on fire and now it's all melted, the yellow plastic drooping down like a sagging eyelid. Young men drive down the road with their music playing loud. They lean out of their car windows and shoot at passers-by with giant water pistols. When they get someone wet they all cheer and laugh. One day they shoot Gloria. She is walking along watching for broken paving stones so she don't trip, and she hears a car with music playing loud and a nice beat. Then she is all wet, a jet of water in her face and shoulder. She stops, startled. She spits and wipes her hand over her face. There is a big cheer. A man is leaning out of a blue car, holding a pink and green water pistol with a huge yellow barrel. The man waves at her and smiles. Then the car drives away fast. Gloria stands still for a bit. Then she keeps walking. The sun dries the water off her top. She decides she don't mind.

One day it's the football. There are loads of men wearing the West Ham colours, light blue and dark red. They wear scarves even though it's hot, because they like wearing all the same colours as West Ham. The big crowd of them floods past the station. They all stand outside the pubs, drinking beer and smoking. Their glasses catch the light when they drink, flashing into Gloria's eyes.

Gloria looks at the faces of all the men for Jack. He might be here today. He goes in the pubs down here sometimes. He likes West Ham too. One time Jack took Gloria in one of the pubs. It's before the summer but the air is getting warm. 'Come with me Gloria,' he says. 'I want to show you something.'

They start walking but he don't take her in the park. She follows him up past the fruit and veg shop, with all the bowls of strawberries and cut pomegranates glinting in the sun, past the bus stop, where the other kids from her college are in a big crowd shouting and laughing. Jack keeps walking, up past where they wash the cars down. The air smells of soap. Gloria sees foam running down windows and black paintwork shining hard.

'Come on,' Jack says. 'You'll like this.'

They go past the church and keep walking, past the bank and the bookshop. They cross the road at the traffic lights.

Jack starts across. Gloria waits for the green man, it's safer. Jack waits for her over the other side of the road. When the man goes green she crosses. The first car waiting at the lights has its roof down, blasting out rap music up loud. Jack takes Gloria's hand. He's never held her hand before.

'In here,' he says. He pulls her with him and pushes open the door to the pub in front of them.

Gloria tries to step back. The room beyond the door is dark. It smells like beer and cigarettes. She hears men laughing.

Jack stops and looks at her. He is still holding her hand. 'In here,' he says. 'You'll like it, Gloria. What's up, you never been in a pub before? Come on.'

He steps in, pulling her with him. Everything goes green at first, because it's so dark inside compared to the sunshine outdoors. The air smells of smoke.

'What you want to drink?' he says.

She don't speak.

'Coke?' he says.

Gloria's vision starts to clear. She can see chairs on the far side of the room, and a bar next to her. A group of men stand holding glasses of beer. They look at her briefly, then at Jack, then they look away.

Jack takes her to the bar. 'Pint of Carlsberg and a Coke please,' he says to the lady behind the bar.

The lady looks at Gloria, then at Jack for a bit. She's chewing gum. 'You alright love?' she says to Gloria.

'She's fine,' Jack says. 'Ain't you Gloria?'

Gloria nods. The woman looks at her a bit longer. Then she shrugs. She gets the drinks and puts them on the counter. Jack pays her and picks up the glasses. 'Come on,' he says. He nods his head in a direction away from the bar. Gloria follows him.

They go through an archway into a bigger room with more chairs and tables and a snooker table in the middle. The room is full of light.

'Look,' Jack says, putting the drinks on a table. 'Look up there.'

He nods at the ceiling, then sits down and lights a fag. Gloria looks up. The whole ceiling is made of glass, crisscrossed over with squares, arching up, coloured glass in red and blue and green patterns of flowers and leaves. She looks at the light coming through, softened by all the different colours. Gloria looks at it for a long time. It looks like the windows of an old church she went to once with Mum, for her uncle's wedding. But that was glass in the windows, not in the roof.

'See, told you you'd like it,' Jack says. 'See.'

He blows out smoke and it hangs in the air like a ribbon, twisting and gliding, catching the light.

'Don't say I never do nothing for ya,' he says.

Gloria thinks about Jack a lot. She wonders what he does. She knows he don't talk to no one else except her. His sister lives down in Custom House but she don't talk to him cos she's an unreasonable bitch. And she's turned his mum against him too. Gloria thinks about his hands on her neck and how it felt. Then she thinks about everything else too, all the times sitting in his house and talking with the window open and the sun coming in.

She keeps walking around and around and going to the parks. People in the street talk to her sometimes. By the Greengate pub a man starts talking to her. He's old and he wears a cap. He asks her her name and what she's doing. Then he talks and talks about what he used to do when he was younger. He used to drive around a lot. He used to pick up his girlfriends and take them to places to have sex. There was one girl he loved a lot but she married a different man.

The man walks with Gloria into the park. He wants Gloria to sit with him. The man says his name is Len. He says he's going to look for Gloria in this park every day, cos he likes her company. He keeps on touching her arm when he talks. He says he gave up smoking because he has poorly lungs.

She tries to walk away but Len walks after her fast. He says, 'Slow down Gloria, I'm trying to talk to you, I'm an old man you know.'

He stays next to her and keeps talking about the ladies he loved when he was young, and how they had sex in his car. When he talks, spit flies out of his mouth and lands on Gloria's cheek.

'Sit down here Gloria,' he says. 'Sit down with me. Talk to me for a minute, make an old man happy.'

It's hot and the sky is white and pressing down. Gloria is so sweaty it feels like the air is sticking to her skin. She sits down beside him. A pigeon pecks near her feet, grey with bits of green and purple shining in its feathers. Across the way there's a group of girls from her college. They are sitting perched on the backs of the benches, drinking bottles of Oasis and laughing loud. They share a cigarette between them. When one girl leans over to hand the cigarette on, the next one takes it as though she is so used to people giving her things to share she don't even have to think about it. Take some and pass it on. When Gloria and her mum go to church sometimes it's like that. They have the bread in a basket and the Ribena in a cup and they pass it around and you take a little bit and pass it on. Gloria likes the songs. They haven't been for a long time though.

Len keeps pushing his hand on Gloria's leg. She don't like it. His hand is really hot and heavy. He's wearing a jacket and his cap. Gloria can smell his sweat when he leans into her. He smells wet and rotten.

She pushes his hand away. He grabs her leg harder, squeezing his fingers into her. It hurts.

'What's wrong?' Len says.

'No,' she says, pushing against his arm.

He keeps on squeezing her leg.

Gloria shouts at him. 'Get off!' She pushes hard and shouts hard.

He lets go. He looks at her surprised. His mouth is a little bit open.

'Get off, fuck off, fuck off!' Gloria shouts and shouts. Off fuck off fuck off! She stands up and shouts more.

Len stays sitting down on the bench, looking at her. The girls from her college are looking over from across the grass. The boys stop playing football and look. One boy jogs towards her. 'Hey,' he says. 'You okay?'

He is about the same age as Gloria. He is tall and thin. Gloria don't answer. She turns around and walks away. The boy don't follow her. Len don't follow her either. Len stays on the bench.

Gloria goes to Jack's place.

5

Jack is leaning out his window, smoking a fag. Gloria sees smoke fly into the air when he blows out. He's wearing a white vest. The tattoos on his arms are dark ink, all smudged.

When he sees her he puts his hand up as if he's going to wave, but he keeps his hand still. Then he takes the cigarette out of his mouth. 'Gloria!' he calls. He sounds happy. He is smiling.

Gloria looks up at him.

'Wait,' he says. 'I'll come down.'

She waits outside the door. She watches the sunlight twinkling on the little bits of broken glass on the pavement. There is a string of brown cassette tape in the gutter. It flickers in the breeze, shining and flashing where it catches the sun. She can hear Jack's footsteps on the stairs. Then Jack opens the door. He stands aside.

Gloria walks past him, into the little dark corridor with the staircase. Everything goes green. She can't see anything for a moment. It's cooler in here.

Jack steps forward and puts his arms round her in a hug. He smells of sweat. It's not like Len, it's sharper. Salt and vinegar. Gloria likes that on chips but not when it's people smelling. She don't move. Jack lets go. 'Up you go then,' he says. 'What you waiting for?'

Gloria walks ahead of him, up the narrow steep steps. The carpet is all bunched up and bloated under her feet. Jack follows. She can smell his sweat and the smoke from his cigarette. At the top of the stairs the door to his room is open.

She goes in. The windows are open and the sunshine is coming in really bright. She thinks the place looks cleaner than before, but maybe it isn't. Maybe it's just the same. The TV is on, a man and a woman talking.

Jack comes in behind her. He shuts the door. 'How you been?' he says. He walks to the window and chucks his fag out.

Gloria don't speak.

'Like that is it,' Jack says. He is twitching, shaking, running his hands over his short short hair. 'Sit down for fuck's sake,' he says, 'you're making me nervous just standing there like a fucking spastic.'

Kinspastic kinspastic.

Gloria goes to the chair and sits down. Jack turns the TV off. The room is quiet.

'Drink?' Jack says. He gets a Coke out the fridge and

gives it to her.

'Thank you,' Gloria says.

'You're welcome. See?' he says. 'Not so hard is it? We're okay ain't we?' He looks at her. 'Well you come round, you can't be that cut up about it,' he says. 'You're still alright with me ain't you? Not sulking about before. Cos you're just overreacting. You know. If you are pissed off.'

Even though he told Gloria to sit down cos it was making him nervous, he is pacing, walking up and down. He runs his hands over a pile of letters on the table, shuffles them out like playing cards, then pushes them back into a stack again. He keeps walking up and down. Gloria stays quiet. She still thinks about what he did when he put his hands around her neck. But she likes being with him all the other times.

'Fucking hell, Gloria,' Jack says. Then he goes and leans against the wall by the window.

He rolls another fag. He keeps turning his head and looking over his shoulder along the street. Gloria looks at the way the light glances off his arm, giving him a gleaming white outline.

'Fucking hell,' Jack says again, shaking his head, concentrating on his cigarette. He licks the paper. 'You're driving me mental,' he says, pointing at Gloria with his lighter. He clicks the lighter a couple of times to get it to light. He breathes the smoke out the window. 'Want some?' he says after a while, reaching towards her with the cigarette in his hand.

Gloria shakes her head. She thinks of the girls in the park

and how they pass their cigarette from lip to lip.

'I missed ya,' Jack says. 'I thought you'd turned against me and all. That you just think I'm an horrible useless cunt like everyone else does.'

Anorrible useless cunt.

Gloria sips her Coke, cold and sweet and sharp on the back of her throat. She still don't say nothing.

'Will you come back tomorrow?' Jack says. 'Will you come and see me again tomorrow?' He is watching her, the smoke drifting up over his face and floating out the window.

Gloria nods.

Jack smiles at her. He keeps smoking his cigarette, smiling. When it's finished he chucks it into the street. He throws himself onto the bed, laying down propped on one elbow, looking at her. 'I like it when you're here,' he says. He lies back and looks at the ceiling and goes quiet. The voices on the telly speak in the background, flat and meaningless.

Gloria sips her Coke. A car passes in the road. Jack lets out a big peaceful sigh. She can hear a bird somewhere outside. She stretches her legs out. A breeze comes and touches her. She likes it too. Her and Jack.

'I can relax now you're here,' Jack says. He's talking quietly, looking at the ceiling. 'You're nice and peaceful.'

Gloria likes the way his voice goes deep and soft. She thinks it would be nice to lay on the bed and listen to his voice and he could sit in the chair. But she don't move. She's tired from the park and from getting away from Len.

An ice cream van plays its song outside, slow and warm

coming through the window. Children's voices.

Jack sits up. 'Want an ice cream Gloria?'

She don't speak.

'A 99 yeah? With a flake? Same as me yeah?'

She nods, looking at him.

'Alright, wait here.' He jumps up. He looks around the room until he finds his wallet, shoving the papers around on his table. Moving fast and urgent like he's in a boxing match. 'Wait here girl,' he says, pointing his hand at her with his wallet clutched in it.

Gloria waits. He leaves the door open. She waits and listens for him on the stairs. She listens to the kids outside. After a bit she hears his footsteps coming back up. He comes in holding two ice creams and gives her one. She licks it. Cold and creamy.

'See, I ain't so bad am I?' he says. He sits down on the bed and eats his own ice cream. After a bit he laughs. 'Might as well enjoy it while it lasts,' he says. 'Less than five months and there'll probably be no refrigeration.'

Gloria's ice cream is dripping on her hand. She licks it off.

'All these fuckers'll be losing their minds,' Jack says.

6

The next day, Gloria and her mum go to her nan's house because it's her nan's birthday. All Gloria's family are there. The day after that it rains. Gloria don't like going out in the rain. She don't like it when she has to walk somewhere in the rain and all her trousers get wet. Soggy around her shins and the back of her knees. She stays indoors. She eats her noodles from her favourite mug and watches the lightning from her bedroom window. She don't have a wash. When Mum gets home Gloria goes to give her a hug, and Mum says, 'Oh, you stink Gloria, go and have a bath.' But Gloria can tell she is pleased.

The next day the sunlight is really bright coming in her window. It wakes her up early. She can hear birds singing and one car passing in the street, the sound lazy and slow like someone drawing a long sweeping line through the morning with a thick black marker.

Mum is still in bed. Gloria has a wash while she waits for her to get up. Then when Mum is having breakfast Gloria makes her a cup of tea. Mum kisses her on the cheek. 'Thank you Gloria,' she says.

It's a good morning.

When Mum's gone, Gloria goes outside. The pavements are all clean from the rain. Gloria scrapes her shoes over the ground. It's red tarmac with little bits of stones poking up. She likes the crunchy scraping feel. The sun is already hot on her head. She's wearing her T-shirt but her arms ain't even cold.

She walks all the way to Jack's in the sunshine, down Barking Road, over the hill past the Greenway, past the church, past all the shops and pubs and up to his road. She presses the buzzer for his flat.

Jack looks down from the window, his head poking out above her. He ain't wearing a top.

'Gloria?'

She looks up at him, squinting her eyes because of the bright sunshine.

'Come up,' he says, and his voice is low, not happy.

He buzzes her in and she opens the front door. She goes inside to the dark hall and up the stairs. At the top of the stairs his door is a little bit open. She pushes it and goes in.

Jack is leaning against the windowsill. He's rolling a cigarette. His hands are shaking. He keeps looking at the paper and tobacco, he don't look at Gloria. 'Where was you?' he says eventually.

She don't speak. She can feel the stress coming off him.

He drops the tobacco on the floor by accident. 'Shit,' he says. He puts his thumb in his mouth. Gloria hears him biting his nail, his teeth clicking as they hit against each other. 'I thought you wasn't gonna come back,' he says.

Jack wipes at his head then he picks up the tobacco from the floor and makes his cigarette. He sticks it in his mouth. His lighter won't light so he shakes it and keeps clicking it, scrape scrape scrape then the hiss and the flame when it finally works. He takes a deep pull and breathes a cloud of smoke out the window. Gloria can smell it.

'I wondered where you was,' he says. 'Do you hate me or something?'

She looks at him. 'No,' she says.

'I thought you was mad at me,' he says. He turns and looks out the open window, his back to her. An aeroplane goes past, making a loud noise. 'Want a Coke? Get yourself a drink if you want one,' he says, without turning round. The muscles in his shoulders flicker as he moves the cigarette away from his lips and back again.

Gloria goes to the fridge and gets the Coke out. There's cans of beer in there too, and a pint of milk for making tea, and a red label bottle of clear liquid. She looks at the clean white light inside the fridge and feels the relief of the cold, the sweat cooling on her forehead. She rubs the cold Coke can on her forehead, trying to cool down from her walk.

She sits down to drink her drink. She decides to ask him now, while he's smoking and not talking. 'Jack,' she says, 'can we go out?'

He don't answer. He finishes his fag and chucks the butt into the street, then he goes and gets a Cadbury's Creme Egg mug from the cupboard and turns on the tap and fills the mug with water. He drinks it all down really fast. 'So fucking thirsty,' he says, rubbing at his throat. Then he fills the mug up again and comes and sits opposite her, on the fold-out chair. 'You wanna go out?' he says.

She don't speak.

'Where you wanna go Gloria? Come on speak up. It's no good saying that then not saying where.'

'Park,' she says.

He shrugs. 'Can if you like.'

Canifyalike.

She waits for him to stand up and get his keys, and maybe put a top on. She can see his nipples. They are round and pink. He rubs at his chest, scratching away a bead of sweat. He drinks his water and stands up. He goes over to the radio on the table and switches it on and stands there nodding, a bit like he's nodding to the music and a bit like he's nodding as he thinks hard about whether to go to the park or not.

'I'm feeling fucked up, Gloria,' Jack says. 'Do you get that, yeah? We'll go to the park, but if anyone starts shit, if any of them little pricks get too rude or them black kids mouth off or whatever I'm kicking off. You get me?' He holds his hands up like he's backing away from a fight. 'Don't hold me responsible,' he says. 'I've warned you now.'

Then he comes up to her and he reaches out and taps her

chin with his finger, very gently. Stroking his finger on her cheek a little bit. He looks right in her eyes. Gloria keeps looking at him. He smiles like he's remembering a joke from a long time ago.

'Drink your Coke,' he says in the end, 'and let's go if we're going.'

They walk to the park together. Jack still don't wear a top. He smokes all the way there. The smoke looks dusty hanging in the sunshine. There's no breeze to take it away. The pavements shimmer in the heat, the air above the ground wavy and distorted.

When they get to the park Jack sits down on a bench. Gloria sits next to him. There are children on the swings nearby, flitting backwards and forwards, kicking their legs out and jerking up at the top of the arc, making the chains bounce and jangle. Sometimes they go really high and then they let go and fly through the air and land on their hands and knees. They scream and cheer each other.

Then people stop moving. The people come and stand on the grass or the path and they stand still. The boys stop playing football. Some people put on sunglasses. Everyone looks at the sky. There is a lady standing near Gloria and Jack. She has orange hair and brown sunglasses.

Gloria looks at the sky too, but the sun burns her eyes and she shuts them.

The sunlight pressing in on her fades. Her skin gets cold. People make noises, say 'Oh, wow.' A dog is barking. When she opens her eyes it's dark, like it's about to be night, or to be a storm. The birds go quiet.

Jack's arm is around her, laying on the back of the bench. Like he is ready to hug her. 'It's the eclipse,' he says. 'See it Gloria? The sun's disappeared.'

She looks up. There is a shadow on the sun.

'It's the moon,' Jack says.

The park is dark and silent. Everyone is still, looking at the sky. And then the sun starts to come back. The birds start singing. People laugh. Some people clap. The boys go back to playing football. The kids start swinging on the swings again.

Jack wipes his eyes, rubs at them. 'Fucking mental innit,' he says. 'See how quick things can happen? And then it's like they never happened. Proper mad innit, Gloria.'

One of the boys playing football kicks the ball towards their bench. Jack stands up and kicks it back, really high and far, all the way away from where they're playing.

'What was that?' the boy yells with his hands spread out.

'Don't fucking kick it near me,' Jack shouts. 'I'm tryna sit down here and mind me own business.'

Mind meyown bizness. Mindmeyown.

Gloria tenses.

The boy looks at Jack for a bit. Like he is thinking about whether to argue more or not. He shrugs and mutters something and then turns away.

'What did you say?' Jack yells.

The boy ignores him and jogs off to where his friends are standing with the ball.

'What did you fucking say?' Jack yells, but no one is paying him attention no more. He comes back and sits beside Gloria. He's still not wearing a top. Gloria can see the muscles going in and out between his ribs when he breathes. 'See that Gloria?' he says. 'That's everything wrong with this fucking place. People ain't got no respect. I fucking tell you they don't know who they're messing with. He don't know what I can do if I'm pushed, yeah? He's lucky I ain't in a worse mood. I can get fucked up when people are messing with me head you know.'

Edyaknow edyaknow.

He shakes his head, looking over at the boy playing football. 'Fucking sick of fucking people,' he says. 'No one has any respect no more. People are just take take take, take you for all they can fucking get. No one wants to help you out when the shoe's on the other side. Oh yeah they want a handout but when you need something they walk right by you. I ain't got shit. No one gives me shit. No one wants to fucking know. Even my fucking family don't want to fucking know. You know what the joke is, if I was a fucking foreigner I'd be alright. If I was a fucking immigrant and I never done nothing for this fucking country I'd be alright. They'd give me everything then. If I was a woman and I got knocked up and I had a kid I'd get everything for free. Me sister gets a flat cos she's a slag. But no one gives nothing to someone like me. You be a poor white man you ain't got shit. I'm stuck where I am. Can't even get a decent job. I try and try but nobody wants to know. Nobody fucking gets it. I don't hate no one but when you try and try and it just gets thrown back in your fucking face all the fucking time you start to fucking hate people. I pay my taxes. I just want equal treatment same as everyone else. Same as what I'd get if I was a fucking refugee or a fucking single mother. Fuck all of them. Fuck everyone, it's me against the fucking world. Family, friends, they'll all fucking let you down. Yous lot'll see, they'll all fucking see. When this all goes to shit. Whole system comes crashing down around their ears. And I'm the only one who knows what to do. Everyone'll be fucking begging me then. Everyone'll be fucking begging me for help. And I'll be on me own, same as I always have been, on me own. Don't need no one. Good riddance to all these cunts.'

Gloria don't say nothing. Jack's watching the boys playing football and the kids on the swings and his eyes are flicking around really fast, looking at all the different people all around.

'You think I'm a prick going on and on,' he says after a while.

Gloria turns her face up to the sun. She closes her eyes. The sunlight shines through her eyelids, everything bright red and warm. Children screaming and laughing and Jack breathing next to her. Jack keeps letting out sighs like he's going to say something else, but then he don't say nothing.

She opens her eyes and sees the sun bright. She turns to look at Jack. White spots flash in front of her eyes, blotting out Jack's face. Jack turns and looks at her too. There's sweat on his head, beading through his short hair. After a while the bright spots go. Gloria can see the blue plastic of his eyes. There are tears wetting his eyes, just damping over onto his eyelids. He sniffs and wipes his nose with his hand, but he don't wipe his eyes. He don't look sad. It's like he don't even know he is crying.

7

Jack says, 'Come on Gloria, I can't deal with this no more, I can't deal with fucking people no more, I've had enough today.' He moves all twitchy. He moves like a squirrel.

When they get back to his place he stands back and lets Gloria go up the stairs in front of him. She waits for him at his door. He comes up the stairs behind her and reaches over her to open the door, his arm around her shoulder so he can put the key in the lock. Gloria can smell his sweat. He is breathing hard. He's shaking. His arm is shaking where he reaches out to turn the lock. It shakes next to Gloria's ear. Heat is coming off his skin. She don't know why he's breathing so hard when they weren't even running.

He undoes the lock and pushes the door open. Gloria walks in ahead of him. Light is coming in bright through the window. The room is hot and stuffy because the windows were all closed up the whole time they were out. Sweat springs from Gloria's skin. Her T-shirt sticks to her. She pulls it forward off her tummy and chest.

Jack sits down sideways in the armchair with his legs sprawled over one of the arms and his head tilted back. He tips his head back and closes his eyes. He is still breathing really fast, his ribs going in and out.

Gloria waits to see if he is okay. He stays still for a long time. He keeps his eyes closed. He kicks off his old Reebok trainers. His feet stink. The smell of them fills up the room. 'Get me a drink,' he says. 'Coke. Something cold.'

She goes to the fridge. She takes out a can of Coke and gives it to him. He reaches out a hand to take it, his eyes still closed. He don't open it. He lays it on his forehead and then on his chest, stealing the cold from the can.

'You take one for yourself and all,' he says.

But Gloria don't want one. She can imagine the taste, too sharp and sweet, sticking to her throat on the inside. She just wants her mouth empty and clean. She presses her tongue against the flat of her front teeth.

'Open the window would ya?' Jack says. 'You just gotta pull it up. Like push it up. Then do the other one. So we get a breeze through.'

He was cross in the park and she don't want him to get cross again, so she does what he says. She goes to the window and tries and tries to open it, but her fingers are slippy with sweat and they slip off the paint. It feels like the window is meant to be closed, like it always was closed and no one can open it.

After a while Jack opens his eyes. 'Leave it,' he says. 'I'll do it in a minute.' He cracks open the Coke and sits up. He drinks it all down with his head tipped back, gulping. The muscles in his neck move. Gloria wants to touch him a bit, where the sweat beads on his chest.

He drops the empty Coke can on the floor.

'Gloria,' he says. He sits back and looks at her. He opens his arms like he's waiting for her to hug him. Even though she partly wants to touch him, she don't move. She stays where she is. Standing in the middle of the room, looking at him. 'What would I do without you?' he says. 'Eh?'

She don't say nothing. He droops his head sideways.

'Do me a favour Gloria,' he says. 'Get my vodka from the fridge would ya? Bring it over.'

Gloria goes and opens the fridge again.

'It's the big bottle,' Jack says. 'Glass.'

Gloria picks up the red label bottle. The glass is all misty. Her hands leave clear prints where they rub the mist off. She takes it over to Jack and he sits up and reaches out for it. He unscrews the lid and takes a drink from it, twisting his eyes and mouth up.

'Yeah,' he says quietly. 'Right.'

He gets up. He goes over to open the window. The muscles in his back move as he yanks it up. The dirty beige curtain blows into the room a bit, then settles down. Jack goes to the back of the room and opens that window too, the one that looks out onto gardens and the mechanic's yard. A breeze comes through. He wipes the sweat off his forehead with his hand and sits back down. A car blows past in the street and the noise of it fills the room, the vrrrrm of the engine and a snatch of song from the car radio.

Jack picks up the bottle and drinks again. 'Sit down for fuck's sake,' he says.

Gloria sits down on the folding chair by the table. There are all letters and leaflets on the table with lots of words printed on them. She looks at them.

'Pile of shit,' Jack says. 'Bills. Junk.' He does a sharp laugh. He takes a drink from the glass bottle. It looks like water. He wipes his lips with the back of his hand. He drinks more. Bits of the liquid dribble down onto his chest. He wipes them away. When he looks at Gloria his eyes slide away and then back. 'Relax for fuck's sake,' he says. 'Have a drink for fuck's sake.'

For fucksake for fucksake.

Jack thinks everything is for fuck's sake. Sometimes Mum says for Christ's sake and that's Jesus. For fuck's sake don't mean too much. You can go to sleep for fuck's sake and get up in the morning for fuck's sake and go to school for fuck's sake. You can just stick it on the end of everything and make everything happen for no reason. And make everything make you angry.

The sky outside goes dark. A grey light presses in through the open window. Wind moves the curtains. It's raining for fuck's sake. Gloria thinks of the first drops falling on the pavement, spreading into the cement and fading away. She goes to the window to see the rain hit the street. She likes the hot concrete smell of it, the heat rising from the tarmac. The rain is coming down hard and fast. It's covering the pavement and the road, making it all shiny and wet. She hopes the grass over the other side of the road is drinking in all the rain.

'Let's have some music,' Jack says. 'Gloria. Put the radio on. Otherwise I just keep thinking and thinking.'

A car goes past, its headlights casting strands of tinsel along the wet street.

'Gloria,' Jack says. 'The fucking radio. Please.'

She looks round at him. The dark room. Him sitting bent forward, swaying, his body moving ugly. Broken against the air around him. The hard gleam of blue eyes just present in the dark of his face.

'Radio,' he says.

Gloria walks away from the window, into the darkness of the room. She goes over to the radio. She twists the knob and the noise gets louder and quieter and louder. Static and a hint of music. Lightning flashes through the window, a bright jagged line tearing through the sky, disappearing behind the houses. Then thunder, crashing and shaking the day.

'Probably all we get. In this storm,' Jack says. 'Move the aerial.'

Gloria pushes it backwards and sideways. There's a glimpse of music. Then the song comes. You're sweet like chocolate boy. Sweet like chocolate.

She rocks so the room and Jack move with the beat. She looks at Jack and smiles.

'You like this one yeah?' Jack says. 'Come here.'

She goes closer.

He holds out the bottle. 'Have some,' he says. 'Have a bit.'

She don't move.

'It's not nice,' Jack says. 'It's horrible.' He laughs. 'Makes me feel nice though, you get me.'

Gloria waits. She stands there looking at him. He could reach out and touch her, if he wanted.

'God, Gloria,' he says. He looks over at the window, at the rain. Lightning flashes again. Thunder breaks the afternoon. The grey light shines on his face and his eyes gleam. The sweat shines on his forehead. 'God,' he says again, and he shakes his head. 'Come here,' he says.

She don't move.

He reaches out and grabs her arm. His hand is cold and wet. Gloria remembers his hand around her throat, the steady pressure, trussme trussme trussme. She tries to pull her arm away and he holds tighter. 'Come here,' he says and he pulls, pulls her towards him hard.

She trips towards him. She puts her hand out and presses on his chest, feels his sweat-damp skin. He puts an arm around her. He pulls her in so she's on his lap. He squeezes her tight and rests his head against hers. He smells of sweat and the chemical smell of his drink, like perfume or when Mum takes off nail polish.

'God,' he says. 'Gloria. You're so…' then he don't say nothing. Gloria can hear him breathing. In, out. It makes a rasping noise like the radio static. Stuff caught in his chest.

'Come here,' he says again, even though she's already there. She tries to hold herself away from him. It's not a nice hug. It goes on too long. He presses her at the wrong angle, her back arching too far the wrong way. Her lower back hurts.

Jack moves his head down and presses his face onto her chest, her breasts. Gloria can feel wetness through her T-shirt. She pushes him back. Jack's holding her too tight and it don't make no sense and Mum always says—

He looks at her. There's tears in his eyes but he don't look sad. He looks mean and like he's laughing. Like he's laughing at her cos he understands something she don't. She feels the anger build in her.

She pushes him harder. He lets go. She falls backwards, onto the floor. The floor is dirty. Little flecks of grit stick into her hands as she scrabbles to get up.

She backs away until she is standing by the window. She looks at him. He watches her. He smiles.

Outside the rain stops. The storm is finished.

Jack gets up and leans on the table. He snaps the radio off. 'Doing my fucking head in,' he says.

He gets another Coke out the fridge. He cracks it open and drinks it, his head tipped back. He finishes the whole can. He looks at Gloria, his eyes hard and bright. He's not smiling or frowning. He's just looking at her like she's another thing in the room, like his table or his chair or the window.

Gloria grips the windowsill behind her. Anchoring herself to the open window and the day outside. The air smells fresh from the rain. The clouds are going away, a bit of sunshine coming back.

Jack turns on the TV. On the screen there is a woman's face, talking. Her voice fills the room. Jack presses the button for Ceefax so he can see the time. 'Four o'clock,' he says. He switches the TV off again with the remote, then he tips his head back and looks at the ceiling.

The room is quiet after the woman's voice has filled it and then emptied it again.

'Let me tell you a story,' Jack says. 'Do you know this story? It happened in America. Not too long ago. It's all true, this story. So there was these two boys and nobody liked them. Everyone in their school didn't like them. No one talked to them. People took the piss out of them. How old are you again?'

He stares at Gloria. She don't speak. He already knows she's nineteen. She already told him before.

'These boys are about seventeen I think,' Jack says. 'Bit younger than you. Everyone treats them like shit. And they just take it and take it. They go into school every day and they walk along the corridors. They go to their lessons and that. People don't like them for whatever stupid reasons. For being ugly or awkward. Or cos girls won't go out with them. You know what kids can be like. You know what cunts people can be.

'But these boys have guns though. See in America you can have guns. And these boys have guns. So that – that changes things. Can you see how that changes things, Gloria? These lads think about what they're gonna do. They plan it. Then one day they go into their school, where no one likes them and no one talks to them, and they shoot everyone. They shoot loads of people. They walk up and down the halls and they go into classrooms and they shoot people. Shoot all the kids in the school and shoot at the teachers. Everyone hides from them and runs from them. All crawling under desks and hiding in cupboards. Everybody'd listen to whatever they wanna say now, you can bet. But they ain't really talking no more. Then it all finishes. And they shoot themselves. The boys do. They die in the school too. And everyone says things. Like some people say you shouldn't be allowed guns, and some people say they was evil little fuckers. And then other people say they was depressed or they was bullied, and no one talked to them and that's why they shot people.'

He's not looking at Gloria no more. He's looking behind her, out the window. Not into the street but up, into the sky.

'Maybe they was evil little fuckers,' Jack says. 'Maybe that's why no one talked to them. Maybe that's why everyone hated them. Maybe people felt it in them. Something really fucking dark. Waiting. Maybe it's not… the one that caused the other. You know?'

He waits. Gloria don't speak. She holds on tighter to the windowsill. She pinches her tongue between her teeth and holds it sharp. She don't like how he's talking, what he's saying, strewing pictures of dead children in her head.

'Anyway, the point is they done it,' Jack says. 'You can't change it. You can't take it away from them. If it was something already in them that made them do it, or something people made them like. They done it. They didn't just talk about it, they done it. And it'll happen again. Other kids'll do it again. Other schools. They didn't… they just fucking went ahead and did it. I don't think they need a load of people feeling sorry for them. Or saying how bad they are. They just done it. They made it into a fact. Goes down in history.'

Then he looks at Gloria, his eyes on hers, calm and serious.

'It was all on the news,' he says. 'It really happened. These kids. Fucking mental, really fucked up and nasty, but it takes guts. Takes guts. To just blow everything off like that.'

They keep watching each other.

Jack's eyes are bright. 'Get me another Coke, would ya,' he says.

She don't move.

'Gloria,' he says.

Don't boss me, she thinks. Don't boss me around.

Gloria don't like this talk no more. Kids getting shot. Jack's angry eyes glaring around the room. Turning the music off and telling her to do this or do that and grabbing her and pulling her too close when she says Stop. She wants to go now. She wants to go home.

She walks over to the door. The door is glossy white paint, chipped in places where someone might have kicked it or punched it. Scratched with slipped keys. There is a metal lock you have to twist to open the door. Gloria turns the lock. The door opens a tiny bit.

Jack stands up and moves, lurching across the room. He falls against the door, pushing it shut. The metal lock clicks closed. Jack leans on the door, his back to it, looking at Gloria. She looks at his bare chest, the hair poking out of his armpit. 'Don't go,' he says. 'Don't go Gloria.'

But she don't like it no more today. She's had enough of him. She remembers his hands on her neck before. She wants to go. 'Yes,' she says. She twists the lock again.

'No.' Jack grabs her hand and pulls it away from the lock. He pushes her hand down towards her side. His fingers are cold. His grip is hard and strong. His thumb pinches, digging in, flattening flesh against bone.

Don't go don't go Gloria.

She screams. One scream, a noise. Short, high-pitched. She wants to make him cover his ears.

Jack looks at her hard, his eyes hard. 'Don't,' he says. 'Stay.'

He is holding her hand like he's holding it nice, like couples do. But his grip is too hard, squeezing and hurting.

Gloria screams again. Louder, and for longer. Jack jerks her arm. 'Shut up will ya!' he says. He says it really fast and hissing. His face is pushed right up close to her face. His eyes bright blue. He screws them up, staring into her.

Gloria looks at him and she don't scream no more.

'You think I don't mean it?' Jack says. 'I really fucking mean it. Scream and I'll hurt you.'

She don't scream. Jack keeps staring.

Then he relaxes a bit. Slowly he pulls his face away from her. He stands upright and looks down at her. He lets go of her hand. He puts his hands on her shoulders and brushes them gently like he's brushing the dust off a piece of furniture. 'What's all that for?' he says. 'What's all that about?'

Gloria don't say nothing.

'You know we don't need this, you and me,' Jack says. 'We're good.'

He says it like he's telling her something obvious. He waits.

Then he says, 'We're good Gloria, ain't we?' His voice cracks like there might be tears lurking under its surface.

Gloria looks and looks at him. She never had somebody who might really hurt her when she screams. If she screams. She don't want to bite him. She just wants to keep very still and quiet. And not let him. Her breathing is getting fast.

'Sit down,' Jack says. 'Sit down. You're not leaving.'

Gloria stands still. She don't look right in his face. She watches his body, his shoulders. She watches to see when he will move. They are both still for a while.

Then he reaches out and grabs her. Grabs her hard by the shoulders. His hands dig in, hard and bony. Soft flesh bruise. Jack pushes her hard over to the armchair. She walks backwards or else she'll fall. He pushes her down into the chair. She can't stop him. She can feel all the power of his arms. It's like she's falling. She lands in the armchair. His face right in hers.

'You ain't going nowhere!' he says. 'You ain't leaving me.'

Gloria cries. The tears tears tears make everything blurry. She can't be quiet no more, it's too much. She cries loud.

She covers herself with the noise and the tears and hides beneath them like a blanket so she can't see or hear nothing and nothing matters except the breathing and the sobbing and the making noise. She screams and screams and cries and cries and all she can think about is the screaming and crying and she don't think about nothing else.

'Gloria!' Jack says.

She screams louder so she can't hear him. Her throat is sore. She hides inside her throat, feeling the pain and nothing else. She feels his hands on her shoulders and she wriggles further into her throat and makes the tears and noise blanket even thicker and more solid so he can't get through.

GloriaGloriaGloriaGloriaGloriaGloria.

He puts his hand on her back. Gloria presses forward, her face in her lap, so no one can see her and she can't see no one. She is folded up tight, covered in noise. Jack's hand on her back. She sucks herself away.

'Gloria. Gloria. Gloria. Gloria. Gloria!'

Then he's got her. Grabbing her by her shoulders and the back of her T-shirt, pulling her, up and forward. The blanket of noise and tears breaks. Gloria can see the room and his legs in jeans and the dirty floor, the sunlight landing on it in patches. The noise stops. The blanket is gone. She stops for a moment. Then she screams louder. Jack pulls her towards the bed. He's strong. She tries to fight on his arms but she can't. He's so strong and she can't do nothing. Like being little. He pushes her and throws her and she lands on the bed, the bounce and give of mattress beneath her. The bed smells of old sweat. He grabs her arms before she can curl up. He pushes her arms back and holds them tight above her head. Pinching the skin and flesh of her wrists against her bones. He leans over, one leg on the bed pressing her legs down.

'Shut up!' he says. 'Gloria! Shut up.'

She screws her eyes up tight.

'I ain't gonna fuck you,' he says. 'Just shut the fuck up will you!' He screams a little bit at the end of his sentence. Like her noise is hurting him.

Gloria goes quiet. Lying all stretched out and pinned down it's no good. She twists and kicks and tries to turn away. Jack keeps onto her. Gloria starts the noise again. To hold him out and away.

'Quiet,' he says. 'Quiet.'

It's a long time. Holding her there. Stopping and starting the noise. Twisting and turning and feeling her wrists pinch and shins bruise from his knees.

Then she lies still and lets the tears dry on her cheeks. She's still scared but her muscles and her throat and her eyes feel tired and she can't shout no more.

Gloria and Jack sit on the bed. They sit in grey-blue shadow, in the corner. They both lean their backs on the wall like it's a sofa. Outside the sun is setting. The sky is striped in orange and pink lines. The colours are nice.

After Gloria went quiet Jack drops his head down to hers. So close their foreheads are nearly touching. And then he lets her go. He sits up beside her on the bed with his legs all drawn up. 'Fuck,' he says.

Gloria knows it's late because it's sunset, and it gets dark really late in the summer. Sometimes after she's gone to bed. So she knows Mum will be having a moment's worry. When she gets home she is gonna be in big trouble young lady. Gloria don't know what her mum will do.

Jack is quiet sitting beside her. Gloria can hear his breathing. It sounds gentle and soft. He don't speak. He don't touch her.

Gloria's skin is itching in the cool air. Her feet are itching inside her shoes.

'I got a feeling, Gloria,' Jack says after a while. His voice is low and croaky. He coughs. 'I got a feeling like this is the last we gonna see of each other. That you won't come back to see me no more.'

Gloria don't speak.

'You'll come back,' he says. 'Won't you?'

She don't speak. She keeps her legs pulled up in front of her, the same as how Jack's sitting.

'Course you will,' he says. 'We're mates, you and me.'

He looks at her. She can feel his eyes trying to reach into hers. She looks straight ahead.

He coughs again. He stands up and stretches, pushing his arms up and leaning side to side. His jeans sag round his waist. He goes to the table and picks up his tobacco. He leans against the wall by the window and starts rolling a cigarette.

'I never done nothing to you,' he says. He is looking down at the cigarette, at the paper pinched between his fingers.

'I never done nothing to you, you was having a spaz-out, whatever you wanna call it. An attack or whatever. I helped you. Calmed you down. It weren't nothing bad. It weren't like – I never touched you. I never touched you, Gloria.'

Then he looks up at her, his eyes bright blue plastic.

'I been good to you,' he says. 'You know I been good to you. I bought you things – food and drink and that. I never expected nothing in return. You know that. I never put my hands on you. Never once put my hands on you. Never tried it on. I've helped you. Been good to you. Had you round here in my place every other fucking day this summer and never once touched you, have I? You answer me that. Have I ever touched you? Bought you food, bought you drink, made you cups of tea. You should be fucking grateful. So don't fucking look at me like that!'

He shouts the last part. Sudden and loud. Gloria jumps. She stops looking at him. She puts her hands over her ears and presses tight, in case he shouts again. But he don't say nothing else. He stops talking. He's just staring at her.

After a while he says something, but Gloria can't hear what it is. She presses her hands tighter. Never once put my hands on you. She don't want to hear no more. She closes her eyes. All curled in tight. No sound. No nothing. Just black and empty, the wall pressing against her back.

She stays like that for a bit. Then she lets her hands slip away. The sound comes back in. The fire in Jack's cigarette crackling as he breathes in. A car passing in the street. The sound of him breathing out smoke.

He's looking out the window. The orange sunlight makes his face and his chest a soft bright yellow. He glances at Gloria. 'Beautiful, this,' he says, gesturing with his cigarette. 'Come and see.'

No. She stays where she is. She don't want to stand beside him. She can see already, the light and the sky all orange and pink and blue. It's the main thing in the room, the thing your eyes want to look at. The light framed in that window. Him standing in front of it.

He looks away from her again, back at the sky. He pulls on his cigarette and breathes out a jet of smoke. He is like a dragon. Gloria remembers stories where dragons take you and guard you in their cave. Won't let you go.

The light drips off him and turns blue, all the sunshine disappearing. It's dark. It's properly night.

If Gloria goes over to the door again she don't know what he will do. But Mum will be so cross. Because Gloria has to be home a long time ago.

So she gets up. She walks over to the door. Her legs are unsteady, pins and needles bursting through them from sitting curled up on the bed.

Gloria turns the lock and opens the door. She looks at the stairs going down.

Jack comes over. He holds on to her arm, but he don't hold it too tight. He says, 'Please don't leave me, Gloria. Stay. Please stay.'

Gloria don't look at him. She looks over at the window, the dark sky and the yellow lights in the houses opposite, Canary Wharf glowing white in the distance, its light flashing on and off. She don't want to see Jack's face and how it looks. She waits to see if he is going to hurt her tighter. But he don't.

She pulls away from him. She starts walking down the stairs. She can't go fast. She holds onto the walls, her hands pressed out against them. It's dark, dark. She can't see where her feet are going.

She slips. Slides down a few steps. She lands on her feet, still standing up. Her heart is going fast. She's frightened from the fall, and frightened of falling again.

'Gloria!' Jack says behind her. 'Gloria just fucking—'

He comes down the stairs after her. She keeps walking down, slowly and carefully. One step, then stop. Then the next step.

'Gloria!' Jack says. 'Gloria—' At the bottom he grabs her arms again. He pulls her round to face him. 'Where you going?' he says.

'Home,' Gloria says.

'Home?' he shouts. He sounds angry. Then he lets her go. He lets go hard. He pushes her backwards. She stumbles on the rotten carpet. Jack pushes his hands over his head, rubbing them over his short short hair. 'Okay,' he says. 'Okay. Okay. Home. Okay, Gloria. Home.'

Gloria watches him. Her throat is dry. She swallows and the inside of her mouth all sticks together. He don't move. He keeps his hands on his head, pressing in. She recognises the gesture. She does it too. The pressure. So you know where your edges are. Where you break from the world.

She turns away. She opens the front door and steps out.

It's night-time but not all the way dark yet. It's a little bit cold cos she's only wearing her T-shirt and pedal pushers. The air smells of fire. In the sky there's a single star, bright against the soft blue.

Jack comes out after her. He is wearing his jeans and no T-shirt, no shoes. There's goosebumps on his skin. 'You're coming back ain't you?' he says. 'Come back tomorrow.'

Gloria starts walking.

'Gloria,' Jack says. 'You'll come back.'

She can go down to the bus stop. She keeps walking, faster. Her feet finding the rhythm. She don't answer him.

Jack is beside her. He pulls her round. His fingers twist into her arm, holding a handful of her. Tight. 'Gloria!' he shouts. His face is all curled up, angry and scared.

'Don't leave me. You ain't gonna leave me Gloria,' he says. She pulls her arm away but he won't let go. His lips are flickering like he wants to say something more but he don't know what.

Headlights. Yellow in the blue dusk. Shining along the road, dazzling her. She can't see Jack's face properly, just an outline. The headlights come closer. Shining the whole street in yellow. Shimmering on the pieces of broken glass on the ground. Lighting up her and Jack. Jack's eyes are bright, shadows dark in his face. The muscles and the veins sticking out in his arm where he's holding her.

The car pulls over towards them, the light dazzling her. It makes a pool of yellow on the tarmac and on the car in front.

There is a man driving the car. He leans over. The window is open. She sees the inside of his car, grey plastic, soft grey seats, an ornate red and gold box of tissues on the dashboard. The man looks at her, his eyes warm and friendly and worried. 'Are you okay?' the man says.

Jack's grip squeezes around her arm, the sweat from his hand sticking and pinching her skin.

The man is looking at her, then at Jack. He frowns.

Jack pulls her further towards him. She feels the heat coming off his body in the night. The air moving around him as he breathes. 'She's fine,' he says.

Gloria watches Jack's face. His mouth moving, the shape of his eyes and nose and teeth. Silhouetted against the headlights.

The man in the car looks at Jack, then looks back at Gloria. 'You sure?' he says, still looking at her. 'Do you want a lift love?'

'No she don't want a lift,' Jack says. Gloria hears his voice all around her.

The man don't look at Jack. He keeps looking at Gloria. Jack holds her arm tight tight tight. Hurts. It hurts. His fingers pressing into her, pushing pain into her, squeezing, denting, making her feel how much he wants her to stay. She bends her head and twists, trying to pull her arm away from him. 'No,' she says.

'Gloria,' Jack says, like he's telling her off. But she ain't doing nothing wrong. He is. He's squeezing her arm too tight. He's all around her. She can't see him properly, just darkness against the light, moving lines, muscles twisting.

'You're hurting her,' the man in the car says. The man in the car gets still, looking at Jack. His face goes like a round hard stone.

Gloria feels Jack's grip loosen. She feels Jack's attention shift from her to the man. Jack's face is all curled up and squeezed up. She feels things change, the air change, the faintly blowing breeze change direction.

She don't move. She waits. She knows something will happen.

The man is sitting in the car watching Jack. His face is hard and heavy like stone. But it's not screwed up or curled up like Jack's is. It's waiting and still. It's ready.

'Why don't you piss off,' Jack says. 'We're fine.'

The man looks at Gloria. She tries to pull her arm away from Jack but he tightens his grip again, so she is jerked back towards him.

Gloria looks at the man and wipes her eyes with her free hand. She really has to go home and she needs Jack to let her go. Something bad is happening and she wants to go.

'Let her go,' the man says.

'Why don't you mind your own business,' Jack says. 'She's special needs. I'm taking her home.'

The man don't seem frightened by Jack, even though Jack is glaring and pushing his words out. He raises his eyebrows. He looks at Jack's bare feet.

Jack don't say nothing.

The man looks at both of them, Gloria crying and Jack holding her arm. Then he turns ahead and looks ahead, through his windscreen at the road in front of him.

There is no one else. No cars, no people. Gloria watches him look. He grips the wheel and sighs. For one moment he closes his eyes.

Then he opens the door. He gets out of the car. He pushes the door to but he don't shut it. He walks around the back of the car. He stands, looking at Gloria and Jack. The noise of the engine is still going. The headlights shine white-yellow on the tarmac and on the red car in front. The man stands up tall.

Jack lets go of Gloria's arm. Gloria pulls away from Jack, moves away. She can see them both, Jack and the man, standing watching each other.

The man turns to look at her. 'You okay?' he says. He's not as tall as Jack. He is wider, more solid. His shoulders are bigger. Jack looks like lines and sharp angles made of bone. Like he could snap apart.

Gloria don't speak.

'Go home,' the man says to her.

And then Jack pushes his face right up close to the man's. Jack's body is curled forward, his hands at his sides, fists clenched. 'Why don't you fuck off. Get the fuck out of our business,' he says. His mouth is tight. He spits the words out.

The man looks at Jack. His face hardens again but he still

don't look frightened. He swallows. His feet shift on the pavement, adjusting position. He is close to the car. He has Jack in front of him and the car right behind him. He has nowhere to go.

Jack stares at him. Jack's eyes are wide and sparkling. His eyes catch the light. They glisten. Jack's face is strained and tense like he is holding in tears. Gloria is watching. She is crying. Her mouth is all dry and afraid.

The man don't speak. He waits. They are all waiting, all three of them.

Jack is breathing hard. His chest rises and falls, the skin between his ribs going in and out. The tattoos on his arms moving as his muscles twitch. Gloria remembers how Jack grabs her and pushes her on the bed. How strong he is. The bruises on her shoulders.

She remembers—

Jack's hand reaches out. His fist hits. The sound is startling, smack of flesh and bone above the sound of the car engine. The man's head snaps back. He staggers and falls back against the car. He stays upright, the car holding him.

The man pushes forward. He swings and hits Jack. Jack's fists are up in front of him. They are hitting and hurting each other and it's not like Gloria ever seen it before, where she seen people at school fighting the teachers and biting and scratching. Or fighting each other, punch and push and wait to see what damage they are doing, flail and kick while other people watching and keeping score. This is different. Gloria never seen the air break like this before, never seen people want to break each other like this before. Jack keeps saying and keeps saying about fights he been in and how he would hurt someone who disrespected him but she never seen it. She didn't know what it means. She sees fists clench and swing. Eyes screwed hard. Heads hit. The man's shoe on Jack's foot, mashing the soft skin, Jack grabbing him. Jack leaning in. Jack—

Jack reaching, taking something from himself and pushing it to the man. Flash of metal. Jack reaching fist closed gripping hard. Pushing in. Jack leaning in to the man, their two bodies close but nothing like a hug. The man shouting out, the frighten in his voice. Jack pulling back. Taking himself back and away. The man swinging at him but missing. Jack pushing forward again, in and forward. Breathing hard. The voices slow. The words blur. They both say things, both shout both swear. Now it's noise like talking used to be and always was, just noise and shapes of sound coming out. Blood coming out. Blood coming out means more than talking, she understands it. She watches. The man is on the floor, his head against the kerb, the engine still running, the lights on, the inside of the car lit up behind him, waiting for him to get in and drive home.

Gloria don't know if she's crying or if she's breathing, all she feels are her eyes. Watching watching. Small pieces of picture. Jack's hand clenched around it. Blood on his knuckles spotting the tattoo words. Blood on the man's chest and pushing out red. Blood on Jack's bare chest. Spotting and dripping. Jack's ribs going up and down, his eyes watching.

The man watching. The man looking at her. The man try to sit up, push up his hands against the floor and fall back down. The man try to reach his hands to push the blood back inside, but his hands move jerky and slow like they're tired and the blood is slipping all over, the blood is covered his shirt and the blood is puddle. A dark red puddle. The man pale pale pale. His eyes close. Gloria is shouting and crying and screaming. The force of the air and the scream coming out wrings her body forwards and back. She pulls the night in and out because there is no other way to breathe. Jack is standing watching quiet. His mouth a little open. He has blood on his skin. Gloria's noise is the only noise.

Gloria is there forever waiting. There. Not in the room with Jack squeezing out ketchup or opening the fridge for Coke. Not listening and understanding words and sticking them all together in her head. There. Screaming crying breathing on the street. Watching the blood. Watching. Jack standing looking down and watching. The breath and the tears and how hard the night is to breathe. She stops. Hands to her ears, waiting for the world to still. The man to die. The noise to stop.

2000

Everyone screams and shouts. Happy New Year! We made it! Gloria presses into the sofa. Auntie Sharon grabs Pat and kisses him. Fireworks on the telly and screams and bangs of fireworks outside, shouting, cheering, people rattling bin lids. Gloria puts hands over her ears, waiting for planes to fall from the sky.

'It's year two thousand Gloria,' Mum says. 'Not nineteen whatever no more. It's the Millennium.'

The telly shows smoke in the sky all over the city.

'Happy new year Gloria,' says Uncle Steve. 'Is it too much noise?'

Mum's face is pink and happy. She pulls at Gloria's hand. 'Get up,' she says. 'It's a party. Have a drink.'

It's gonna be mental, Jack says.

Gloria's younger cousins are chasing round with balloons. The older cousins are out with their friends. Darryl squeaks the balloon with his fingers. Gloria presses hands on her ears more. Cold air comes in and the outside noise gets louder. Smell of cigarette smoke. Cold breeze. She takes her hands off her ears, listening out for everything breaking. Jack says she should stick with him. Mum said Jack's in prison. And with any luck they'll throw away the key.

'Mother close that door would you. Bloody freezing!'

Gloria's nan comes in from the kitchen. 'Gotta let the new year in and the old year out,' she says.

'New century!'

'Want one Jo?' says Auntie Mel.

'Yeah go on I'll have a cheeky one,' Gloria's mum says. She touches Gloria's face. Her eyes look strange. 'It's alright Glor,' she says, 'it's a party, have fun.' She goes away.

Gloria's nan sits on the sofa. She rubs Gloria's shoulder but she don't say nothing.

The TV is still on, a man talking on the screen. The lights are still working. There is music still playing underneath all the noise. Fireworks outside.

Jack will be outside under all the fireworks, trying to find his gun. Getting his things to take to his place. He will be outside the city hidden in trees, in dark and quiet. Somewhere small. Building a fire.

The light is on. Warm bright yellow. She can hear it buzzing. She can hear the TV buzzing. The house is full of high-pitched noises of things still working. Everyone talking and laughing. Uncle Steve takes an orange crisp from the bowl and puts it in his mouth.

You need to stick with me Gloria. When the shit hits the fan.

Jack is in prison. He is in prison for what he done. Don't worry about Jack no more.

She gets up. She goes out of the room, into the corridor. She wants to see outside and see it all happening, fireworks, see the planes fall. She wants to be out in the cold and dark. The front door ain't shut properly. She hears her mum's voice saying 'What a shit fucking year.' She pulls the door open and Mum and Auntie Mel are standing there outside. Both smoking. Mum blows out smoke. 'Gloria,' she says and coughs. 'You okay?'

Gloria don't speak. Mum and Auntie Mel look at her. The air is full of distant sirens and fireworks.

'I'm just having one cos it's a party,' Mum says. 'You okay? Go back inside, darling.'

A green firework sparkles in the sky.

'Want a hug?' Mum opens her arms and smiles. The smile looks wrong. She smells wrong. She smells like Jack's smoke.

Gloria goes back inside. She sits on the stairs and listens. Nothing is breaking except fireworks.

Jack is in prison. He is locked up in prison. She thinks of him. Inside a room with bars on the door. Outside in the night with a decent rucksack. Looking for somewhere by a river. Looking for crates to make a bed.

2001

1

The room smells like old carpet, like Jack's hallway. It has a TV and blue chairs and a low table. It is court.

Jack is not in the room. Only Gloria and Mum and a lady wearing a big black dress. Gloria is wearing a black shirt and black trousers that Mum got her specially and the shirt pulls and rubs on her shoulders. The TV is in front of Gloria. It is black and empty. Gloria can see herself in it a bit. She sways and sees her shape sway.

'The link'll come on soon,' the lady in the black dress says. She smiles at Gloria. Her lips have red lipstick on.

'Remember what we said, Gloria,' Mum says. 'They'll be on the video and they're gonna ask you questions like the police did, about what happened. And you just gotta answer them.'

The TV crackles and pictures come on the screen. It is

another lady in a black dress. She has white curly hair on top of her hair.

'Gloria,' the lady on TV says. She smiles. 'Can you hear me?' she says.

'Gloria, answer her,' Mum whispers. The lady in the room frowns at Mum and shakes her head.

'Gloria,' the lady on TV says. 'Can you say yes if you can hear me?'

'Yes,' Gloria says. The lady on TV smiles. She says things. Her voice is flat like TV voices. It's not like normal talking to someone where their words are solid shapes that come out of their mouth into the air and Gloria can break them up and stick them together. Find rhythms in them.

'I want to ask you about Jack,' the lady says. All stuck together and smudged into one colour. Even the word Jack sounds like it ain't real. 'Gloria, we saw the video you made with the police,' the flat voice says. The lady's mouth moves up and down.

Gloria's chair is hard. She leans back and puts her legs forward. Mum nudges her.

'Where's Jack?' Gloria says to Mum.

'Don't worry, you ain't gonna see Jack,' Mum says, very quiet. She touches Gloria's hand. The light in the room is yellow. Mum's face looks strange in the yellow, it keeps bending and shifting and Gloria can't see it properly. She looks at the grey marks on the wall. On TV the lady says Gloria. The lady flickers when Gloria looks at her. Gloria stands up.

Dull in the background the flat voice says you police Jack hit. TV is not real. But the lady's saying real things. Her voice don't sound real. Pictures come in Gloria's head that aren't on TV. Night-time and shouting. Car lights shining on blood. Gloria keeps her eyes open and looks at the table and the grey carpet and the wall. She rocks fast to make them move fast and fluid. The lady in the room waves at Gloria and points to her seat. Gloria looks away so she can't see her pointing and she don't have to sit down.

Gloria the woman on TV says. You police she says.

'Sit down, Gloria,' says the lady in black. And Mum reaches out her hand and says, 'Sit down.'

Gloria don't sit down. She looks at the wall.

'It's really important that you try. Can you try?'

'Just listen to the questions, Gloria.'

Questions come in the smudged voice. What did you see Jack do? Gloria closes her eyes and she can see a knife. A man on the pavement. She opens her eyes again quickly. Her tummy moves inside her, sharp sick sliding up her throat and making her eyes burn. The lady on TV is saying things. Jack and stab. Gloria goes close to the TV. She looks for a button but she can't see one. There is a thick black wire leading to a plug on the wall. She holds the plug hard and pulls it out. The TV goes black.

'Oh my god,' the woman in the black dress says. She stands up. Gloria puts her hands on her ears, pressing hard so her elbows stick out. Mum stands up and puts her hands on Gloria's shoulders.

The woman shakes her head and says something. She goes out the room. Mum stays beside Gloria. The woman comes back in and says some more things to Mum. Her mouth is twisted up. She don't look happy. A bit of red lipstick is on her teeth. She opens the door.

Gloria takes her hands off her ears. The woman's saying, 'At the end of the day, if she's not going to cooperate then—'

Gloria goes out the door fast. Mum comes after her.

Auntie Sharon is waiting in the corridor. The corridor has old blue carpet and yellow walls the same colour as the light. Auntie Sharon and Mum look wrong in the light. Mum hugs Gloria. Mum is wearing a black jacket with a shiny black brooch on and the brooch digs into Gloria's cheek. Gloria holds onto Mum tight and presses her face in further, lets the brooch dig into her more. Auntie Sharon puts a hand on her back. The lady in black is talking to Mum and Gloria presses her ear into Mum's shoulder, presses her hand on her other ear. She ain't listening. She closes her eyes tight. Everything gone. All of it. Mum lets her stay like that for a bit then she starts patting Gloria's back to tell her to move. Auntie Sharon pulls Gloria's hand away from her ear and says 'McDonald's?' Gloria pulls her hand back on her ear. She keeps her eyes closed. She wants to go home and go in her room and listen to her Bob Marley CD. Mum pats her back again. She holds Gloria's wrist. 'Home,' she says, loud enough for Gloria to hear it. 'We're going home now, Gloria, okay?'

They walk along the corridor. They go through two yellow wooden doors. The doors have circular windows in them, with small squares made of wire mesh inside the glass. There is a group of people standing in the corridor. Mum stops walking. 'Oh god,' she says quietly. 'I think that's his family.'

'The man who died?' Auntie Sharon says.

'Yeah.' Mum puts her hand on her face.

A girl looks over at Gloria. She stares and stares at her. The girl has a round face. Her eyes are wet and red and puffy, and her face is sad. She has dark red shiny lipstick and a brown headscarf. She walks towards Gloria. 'You saw what happened,' the girl says. 'Didn't you? Why didn't you say nothing? Do you know why they argued?' She's standing tall. Her voice is loud.

A lady comes and stands behind the girl. She looks thin, but not like Jack looks thin. She looks thin like she's sick and the life's being sucked out of her, pulling her skin tight to her skeleton. She looks at Gloria and there's not much of anything in her eyes, they're just blank. She's just looking. Two tall boys come. They are nearly men. One is very tall and thin, his hair gelled in curtains. The other is slightly shorter. He has a thin spiky moustache. They stand beside the woman and the girl.

'I'm so sorry for your loss,' Mum says. The lady nods.

The girl is still watching Gloria. 'Does she speak?' she says to Mum. 'She spoke to the police, right?'

'Sumera, leave her,' says the moustache boy.

The girl starts crying, tears dripping on her cheeks, but she don't make a noise.

'I'm sorry about my sister,' says the moustache boy.

'Don't,' the girl says.

'We need to go,' says the lady. 'Come on, Sumera, Salim. Come on.'

She turns away and the children follow her. She moves slowly and a bit bent over even though she don't look old.

Gloria knows the man Jack killed is called Mr Miah. The police told her. Mr Usman Miah. The children are Mr Miah's children. Sumera. Salim. And the taller boy. The woman is his wife. The girl, Sumera, is crying because Mr Miah is her dad and he's dead. Because Jack killed him.

'Let's go, Gloria,' Mum says. But now Gloria don't want to go. She wants to stay where she is. She wants to watch Mr Miah's family, the tall boys and the girl with the red lipstick and the faded thin woman.

2

Mum says different things on different days.

She says, 'How was you going back to this bloke's house and you didn't think to tell me? Why you been keeping secrets?' She says, 'I can't turn my back for a bloody minute can I?' Her face frowns. Her mouth twists down. 'Chips,' she says. 'All the two of you done is eat chips!' She shakes her head. 'He must of thought all his Christmases come at once when he met you.'

But Gloria and Jack never did Christmas together. Because the whole time she knew him it wasn't Christmas. She thinks what Jack's room would look like with a tree and decorations. She thinks of Jack with a paper crown on his head.

'Christ's sake Gloria,' Mum says. 'You think everyone's your friend?'

Then other days Mum says, 'You get bored, don't you

darling. You need company. You need things to do. You can't spend every day by yourself.'

She says, 'Did Jack ever hurt you? Did Jack touch you anywhere?'

Gloria thinks of Jack grabbing her arm and Jack pushing her on the bed and Jack pressing his face on her chest and Jack touching her chin with his finger and Jack holding her hand. Bought you food, bought you drink, made you cups of tea. You should be fucking grateful.

'We drink Coke,' Gloria says.

Mum looks at her. 'Is that it? You ate chips and drank Coke? Why did you never tell me about him Gloria? All them times I asked? Why'd you never tell me who you was hanging round with?' She holds herself up tall for a moment, then she slumps. She sits down on the sofa. She goes quiet. 'I can't know unless you tell me,' she says. She looks away from Gloria, at the floor.

Another day she says, 'Gloria, listen to me.' She speaks slow and sad. She ain't angry but she ain't smiling. She says, 'Listen to me,' and Gloria turns away and looks at the wall because Mum is looking at her too hard. On the wall is a picture of Gloria when she was a little girl. She's wearing a dress with blue and yellow and green spots on. The dress is a lovely pink-red colour. Gloria is smiling in the picture. She is holding a pink teddy bear. Gloria still has the teddy bear in her room.

'Listen,' Mum says. Gloria don't turn round. 'Some people mean you harm,' Mum says. 'You can't trust people. You can't just trust people. Some people don't wanna be kind. Lots of people are out there looking to hurt you or take the piss outta you or take your money. You can't just go with people. Any bloke coming up to you in the street. You have to be careful. You can't just talk to everyone. I want you to go out Gloria, I want you to do things. But you gotta tell me who you talk to. Otherwise I'll worry. In fact you know what? Don't talk to anyone you don't know. Okay Gloria? You got that?'

Gloria puts her hands on her ears. She rocks, and everything shifts around her, her young-girl self with the smile and the teddy coming closer and moving away.

*

There's nothing to do. She walks around in the summer, but now when it's cold there's nothing. Sometimes Mum takes her out, to the cinema or to see family. One time they go to Southend. They walk by the sea. The sea is grey and brown and has dark brown seaweed and bits floating in it, rushing up onto the pebbles. Gloria's hands and ears get stung by the wind and her eyes cry even though she ain't crying. They buy chips in the shop and Gloria has them with salt and vinegar and she chooses a Coke and drinks it and eats the hot mushy chips.

Mum signs her up to do jewellery making and she goes to the college in Forest Gate once a week and puts coloured beads on strings. She likes it but it's only Wednesdays. She walks around everywhere, even in the rain. She thinks about going to Jack's house but he ain't there no more and she's scared to see the road again and see if the blood's still all there. Mum says Jack is in prison and he'll be there a very long time. He can't hurt you or nothing. You won't see him again.

Mum has a calendar in the kitchen. She crosses through days with a black pen. When a day is finished she puts a line through it. If you look for the first day without a line through it, that's when you are. Except sometimes Mum forgets to cross off days and then Gloria's on the same day over again and then Mum crosses them all off together and three days go at once. It says the year at the top of each page with the number 2001.

There's a clock in the kitchen opposite the calendar. It's dark green with white numbers around the edge. And Mum has another smaller clock in her room by her bed, white and square with rounded edges. It has black lines instead of numbers and thin black hands that flick round like spiders' legs. Gloria can't tell the time. She knows when it's late because it gets dark, but that changes if it's summer or winter. When she went to school they said the day and the date every morning, the month and the year and what the weather was like. But now it's been a long time, lots of days that are all the same as each other. On Wednesdays she goes to the jewellery class and on Saturday and Sunday Mum don't go to work, but otherwise it's hard to tell what day it is. Seasons are easier, hot or cold, and the trees change and the sunlight.

Gloria walks around and finds new parks and new streets. Her hands and her nose get cold and her feet get damp and cold through her trainers. She goes down High Street South and finds a graveyard that is very quiet and big with so many trees like a forest. When she goes in, the buses and the traffic disappear and it's just her own breath and rain dripping. There's no leaves on the trees because it's winter. One time she goes to Jasvinder's house, and she sits with Jasvinder and drinks tea and watches television. Jasvinder's mum sits with them and keeps saying 'How are you Gloria?' and 'What are you getting up to now college is finished?' Gloria don't want to speak to her. She drinks the tea and goes.

She wants to walk and walk because there's a lot of things in her head. Pictures. Mr Miah on the ground, his hands scurrying to hold the blood back in. And Jack smiling and touching her chin. Jack holding her arm tight. All of these pictures make her want to walk and move and get away, and to see the people and pavements and shops and trees around her, solid and happening. Sometimes it's hard to sit down on Wednesdays and concentrate on the beads, on choosing which colour she wants. Sometimes it's a relief when the lesson finishes and she can go and walk and walk and let the pictures happen and go.

One day it's misty, the air is full of cold fine drops and they sink into her, getting under her scarf and inside her hood. Everything is dull, the saris and the fruit less colourful, the shop signs faded. The light is grey and a bit dark like it's evening, but it ain't. She turns off Green Street and goes past all the tower blocks to a small park. The park is not the same one she went to with Jack. It's only got a roundabout and a swing and a bit of grass. She sits down on the bench. It's cold under her bum and legs. She's shivering. Her hood is up, her scarf pulled tight, her hands inside her pockets. She thinks about Jack sitting on the bench beside her with his arm stretched out. There's a girl walking through the park in black trousers and a black jacket and a black headscarf. Gloria looks at the girl. The girl has a round pretty face. She looks sad and serious. Gloria knows the girl. She saw her in court. Mr Miah's daughter. The one called Sumera. She is not wearing lipstick today. Gloria watches her. Sumera will stare at her. Sumera will say You saw what happened. She waits and watches. But Sumera don't stop. Sumera walks past her, out of the park. Gloria gets up and follows.

Sumera crosses the road and goes to a house opposite the park. She goes to the door and knocks on it. The door opens. Gloria is too far away to see who opens it. Then Sumera goes inside and the door shuts. Gloria walks along the street until she is across from the house. She stands and looks. The house is cold and grey. The curtains are thick white net and she can't see anything inside them. The bricks of the house are more grey than brown and the door is black. She stands watching. It's cold deep in her shoulders, it feels like her shoulders will snap from it. She decides she will come back tomorrow. Maybe Mr Miah's family live in that house.

In the morning when she hears Mum getting up to go work she gets up and gets dressed and goes downstairs. Mum says, 'Hello Gloria you're up early.' And Gloria goes out straight away after her cup of tea. It's cold and windy. She sits down in the park. She can see a long way. Across the grass and through the railings and to the house where Mr Miah's family live.

The tallest boy comes out. He is wearing a white jacket and tight black jeans and carrying a thin black drawstring bag. He walks away along the road. Gloria don't know his name. She wants to walk after him but she wants to see who else comes out too.

Sumera comes out. She's wearing the same as yesterday. Black trousers and black coat with a fluffy grey hood. A big black rucksack. She crosses the road and comes into the park.

Gloria's not hiding because she's only sitting down on a bench. She's not hiding and she ain't doing nothing bad but still she don't want Sumera to see her. She don't look towards Sumera. She looks on the ground. The path is grey concrete with little grey stones inside it, sticking up sharp, to cut your hands if you trip over. The stones shine in the rain. Gloria rocks her head a bit to make the glow move around.

A boy comes on a bike. He's riding slow, standing up on the pedals. He's wearing a grey tracksuit. The hood is pulled tight round his face so his face is a circle. He looks like the circle drawings of faces Gloria seen in school, to teach her what happy and sad look like. His eyes are dots and his eyebrows are straight across and his mouth is a small straight line. She don't know what that means. He's not showing any feeling on his face. He stops his bike in front of her. 'You waiting?' he says. He nods when he speaks, jerking his face towards her a little bit. Gloria don't speak.

'You wanna pick up?' he says.

Gloria looks away from him.

He jerks his bike forwards at her legs. 'Boo!' he shouts, sudden and loud.

Gloria gets up. He laughs, a noisy sharp burst. His face is still not showing any type of feeling. Just lines and dots. She puts her hands on her ears so it don't matter if he shouts again.

She walks away. Sumera is ahead, out of the gate, walking down the street under the big tower blocks.

Gloria walks along with her hands still on her ears, fast because of the boy but not too fast to catch up Sumera. She reaches the park gate.

Ahead of her, Sumera takes something out of her pocket. It's a small packet and she unwraps it and drops something on the floor and puts something in her mouth. She is still walking at the same time as unwrapping the packet, moving fast. Gloria stops and looks behind her. The boy is gone, over the other side of the park, turning slow circles with his bike. She takes her hands off her ears. Sound rushes back in, a dull grey hum of cars and engines and voices and drills and sirens and aeroplanes. Gloria walks down the street after Sumera. The thing Sumera has dropped is a shiny blue spot on the ground. When Gloria gets closer she sees it is paper from a chewing gum packet. Gloria picks it up and puts it in her pocket.

In the pound shop she stands in front of a row of boxes. The lights in the pound shop are very bright and not yellow, so she can see the colours properly. The boxes are cardboard and bright colours. She tries to decide which is her favourite. She wants to choose the best one. There is a red glittery shiny one like Sumera's lipstick. But it's like blood as well. There is a bold blue sparkly one. There's a gold one. There's a pink one with all different colours in it when you move your head and let the light show you. There's a blue-green one the same. When Gloria moves her head there's gold and orange and blue and red caught on the surface of the box, sitting just above or just under the pink and the green. There and then gone again. She touches the blue-green box with the colours trapped in it. The surface is all bubbly and she presses it to feel if it will crinkle but it don't. It's smooth and bumpy together. She chooses it. The blue-green looks like the sea in pictures.

She buys the box and takes it home and puts the blue chewing gum wrapper inside it.

3

One day it gets warmer. There's sunshine and Gloria don't need her coat. She goes to the park to see Mr Miah's family. Gloria's got a lot of things in her box now. She's got the wrapper Sumera dropped and she's got a pebble from the front of the house where the family live. She's got a bit of mud that came off the bottom of Salim's trainer, the moustache boy. The mud has dried and crumbled now so it's just lots of brown crumbs of earth inside the box. She's got a receipt the faded lady dropped, Sumera's mum. She has a lighter that the bigger boy put down on a wall and forgot about, yellow plastic with a little metal wheel at the top. When she sits in the park the boy on the bike is there sometimes but he don't come up to her no more. Sometimes he meets people and talks to them low and huddled. She sits and sees the family coming and going. The mum is always gone before Gloria gets there in the morning, and she comes back to the house last in the evenings. It's dark when she gets back. Sumera and Salim usually go out of the house close together. The older boy goes at different times on different days. The house don't always look grey. Sometimes when it's night-time and the lights are on inside it looks warm and yellow-orange all around the windows. Sometimes she can see the TV through the net curtains downstairs, a blue-green glow with lots of moving colours in it just like the box she chose. She can hear the family shouting and laughing inside.

The sunlight is in the park and shining on the grass so the grass looks green and shiny like a pool of water. There are round yellow dandelions on it. The sun is shining on the trees so when the leaves move in the wind they look like the sea with bits of sunshine moving and flickering all over it. Gloria stares and stares at the trees and the way they move and look like the sea. They have leaves on them so it is spring. Winter is finished and summer is coming next. She looks over at the house. Today in the sunshine the bricks look more yellow than grey, a warm brown-yellow. The windows shine. It looks like a nice house, a happy house. She wants them to be happy. She thinks about it a lot. Mr Miah and Jack and the blood. The knife shining. Mum is still cross with her about it. She still says Have you spoke to anyone today Gloria? Have you been round anyone's house? She still says How can I trust you? But Gloria ain't spoke to no one and she ain't been in their house, she's just sitting on her own and walking on her own. Sometimes a man comes and says Hello to her or a different man says Hey sexy or another one asks her for money. Sometimes a woman comes and says Spare any change? And Gloria don't speak and walks away. Even if they shout.

The tallest boy comes out of the house. He is wearing a thick cream-coloured jumper and black jeans. He walks down the road, flickering through the railings.

Gloria gets up. She walks out of the park and turns to follow him. She walks slow. Walking fast is too hard and she can sometimes fall over. He's ahead of her, the ribbed cream knit of his back. It would feel nice to touch. Soft and warm.

He turns the corner onto Barking Road. She follows. Barking Road has lots of buses and cars and shops. The boy is in front of her, the pavement between them, the stalls of fruit and vegetables and the bus stop and a man with a big dog on a lead and the yellow and blue sign for the Blockbuster video shop swinging slightly, tipping light back and forth into Gloria's eyes.

The tall boy walks down past the pub that she went in with Jack and waits for a break in the traffic. He crosses the road just as Gloria gets there, just before the green man comes. Then Gloria crosses too. Now she is a bit closer to him. He goes past the bank, past the church and the car wash and more houses and shops. He turns up Greengate Street and walks along the street for a bit, then he crosses over the road. He just runs over the road when there's no cars coming. He don't go to a crossing. Gloria walks up to the crossing and waits till it's safe. She can still see him over the road. He goes in the park. It's the park she goes to with Jack a lot. The green man lights up and she goes across the road. She walks into the park. The tall boy is ahead of her, down the path. He goes past the big slide and walks along next to the grass.

A man with short hair is sitting on the bench she and Jack sit on. It might be Jack. She looks and looks at him. He has his head turned away so he is looking towards the cherry blossom tree. The tree has puffs of light pink blossom all over it and whenever a breeze blows the blossom flutters down like snow. The man is watching, looking at the pink blossom against the blue sky. He is wearing jeans and a black jumper. She ain't seen Jack wear them clothes before. The man is fatter than Jack but his hair is short like Jack's. She walks closer to him. He turns around and she sees the side of his face and it ain't Jack. Sometimes that happens, she sees Jack walking past her and looks and it's not really him. So she don't feel sad because she's used to it. And Jack is probably in prison still.

She looks ahead to the tall boy. He's turning down the path near the old fountain. The fountain is covered in green slime like bogeys and it's full of old cans and crisp packets that shine bright silver in the black water. There are orange flowers planted round it. There is a man and a woman sitting on a bench, both drinking cans of beer. Gloria knows them because Jack knows them and he says hello to them and talks to them sometimes when Gloria's with him. They both nod at her. The woman says, 'Alright dear.' Gloria nods at them.

They know she don't like speaking a lot because Jack tells them once.

The tall boy goes to the basketball court. Gloria walks along after him but she don't go all the way to the court. She sits on a bench. There's no one else sitting on it. It's made of metal covered over in thick green rubbery paint. There's lots of regular oval holes in the metal and people have picked and peeled at the green paint so you can see the silver underneath. She rubs her finger along the edge of a broken blister of paint and pulls at it. A piece peels upwards. She pulls some more so there's a strip of grey metal. She looks over towards where all the boys are in the basketball court. The tall boy is walking towards them. There is a brown diamond-shaped leather patch sewn on the top of his cream knitted sleeve.

'Hey Tariq, wassup,' one of the boys yells. They touch fists.

Tariq is his name. He turns so his face is in the sun, his hair shining. He is smiling. His face looks happy. He talks to the boy who shouted his name. The boy is wearing a light-blue tracksuit and a gold necklace. They are talking quietly. Then another boy in a light-grey hoody comes up to them and talks and Tariq shouts out 'Fuck off man' loudly but he's laughing at the same time, the laughter bubbling through his words. He pushes the boy and the boy pushes him back and pulls him into a headlock. Gloria watches. She don't want the boy to hurt him. Tariq pushes the boy off and pulls him around in a headlock then they break apart laughing and it's all just a game, they are playing, no one has knives. And Tariq runs with the other boys. He is taller than a lot of them. He gets the ball and jumps and puts it inside the hoop and the boys shout Yes Tariq! Tariq's dad Mr Miah tried to help her. So if anything happens Tariq will probably try to help her too. Someone might come up to her and tell her to move or to give them money but Tariq will help. Gloria's own dad went away when she was little. She don't remember him. Her mum don't talk about him much. Gloria's seen a photo of him. He's wearing a stripey T-shirt in the photo, with dark pink and red and white stripes going across it. He's smiling. His hair is very short.

Tariq runs and plays. Even though he's tall he's young. Gloria keeps watching and watching. A cold breeze comes. The sun starts to set. The clouds turn pink like the colour of the cherry blossom. One of the boys picks up the ball. The boys touch fists and walk away in different groups. Tariq is with the blue tracksuit boy. They walk away from the court, towards Gloria. They stop at a bench near her and huddle up together, leaning together, their heads almost touching. Tariq puts his hands out to shield something, so Gloria can't see what they've got. Something flashes from his pocket when he leans over. After a bit they get up and walk towards her again. The blue tracksuit boy is smoking and he passes it to Tariq and Tariq smokes too. Then Tariq passes it back to him. Gloria can smell it's weed. They are close now. Tariq looks at her. Then he stops. He stares right at her.

'You alright man?' says the blue tracksuit boy to Tariq. He is shorter than Tariq and his hair is shaved short at the sides and sticks up on top. He has a shiny stud in his ear. Gloria looks at Tariq's jumper. The cream ribbed wool. There is a zip down the front. It looks clean and warm.

'It's you innit?' Tariq says to Gloria.

'What, you know her?' says the tracksuit boy.

Tariq keeps looking at Gloria. Gloria looks at his face. He's frowning. She looks at his jumper some more. She really wants to touch it. There is a brown leather tag on the zip.

'I knew it was you,' says Tariq. 'You been watching us innit? I seen you.'

Gloria don't answer. She taps her hands on her ears so the sound turns on and off.

'Bruv who is she?' says the blue tracksuit boy. 'Bruv I swear she's special.'

Tariq keeps on looking at Gloria. Gloria looks at him. There is sunset light in his eyes making them shine warm brown.

'You got to stop following us man,' he says softly. 'You hear? We don't like it yeah.'

'Who is she?' the blue tracksuit boy says again.

'She was there when my dad got killed innit.'

'Oh shit.'

Kil dinit kil dinit.

Tariq looks at Gloria again. His face goes sad and serious like Mr Miah's did, but not hard, not like stone.

'Come man,' Tariq says. Tracksuit boy passes him the joint and he pulls on it. Gloria hears it, Tariq's breath sucking in and the crackle of flame, she hears it in front of all the noises in the park of children playing and shouting and dogs barking and the traffic going by outside. Tariq and his friend walk away. She watches them go, blue and cream side by side under pink cherry blossom.

She goes to the bench where Tariq and his friend sat together. Where the thing flashed out of Tariq's pocket. It's there on the bench. A silver key. It has a circle at the top and then a long bit with different triangles and bumps along the edge. Gloria's own key is different. It's gold and dull where she's touched it and touched it to open her house, and it has a square shape at the top. Tariq's one is very shiny. She picks it up and puts it in her pocket.

4

Tariq's key is heavy in the blue-green box and it slides around and knocks and makes a lovely soft thud against the side of the box. It feels like the box has something real and important in it, not just rubbish and mud. She slides it and listens to the noise a lot. Then she takes the key out and looks at it. She wipes her thumb across the silver circle to make it shine more.

Gloria don't go out for a bit because she's got a bad period. She stays at home and stays in her room and listens to her Bob Marley CD. She opens the window and the sky is warm and bright and she sits down beside the bed, listening to the songs over and over. Tipping the box to make the key thud. She feels happy and aching, she aches deep inside because she wants to be outside, walking on the warm pavements and sitting in the park, hearing the trees move.

And she knows it's summer and she can do that a lot, for a lot of days before it's winter again.

The day she feels better it's Saturday. On Saturday she helps Mum with cleaning and they sometimes go shopping but Gloria hates the supermarket and she puts her hands on her ears and closes her eyes a lot so mostly Mum goes by herself. But this day Gloria gets up and she has cornflakes and she has a cup of tea, and Mum says, 'We should go out today. It's a lovely day outside.'

It is bright. The sunshine is coming through the window and lighting up the calendar.

'I wanna see where you go,' Mum says. 'Maybe we can go together? You can take me to your favourite park and we can go for a walk. What about that?' Gloria don't speak and Mum says, 'Gloria I'm asking you a question. You wanna go for a walk together?'

'Yeah,' Gloria says. It comes out short and sharp. She plays it over and over, her own word, yehyehyeh, and rocks a bit with the rhythm.

Mum smiles. 'Okay. Get dressed then.'

They go to West Ham Park. Gloria don't want to take Mum to the park she goes to with Jack. And she don't want to take her to the park where the family live. So they walk around the rose garden and the squirrels run around the benches and run up trees. They don't talk much. Mum is smiling and looking away from Gloria, at the flowers and the sky. They walk past the children's playground with all the screaming and laughter and running. They walk on the paths through the grass. There are people playing cricket. There is an ice cream van.

Mum says, 'Let's go to the cafe shall we? Treat ourselves.' They walk all the way out of the park towards Stratford and go to a little cafe with a red sign. Mum gets them cups of tea and she gets some toast. She puts the plate of toast in the middle of the table.

Gloria takes a piece and then Mum does. The toast tastes salty and oily and the tea tastes hard and clean.

'I wanted to talk to you about something,' Mum says. 'Been thinking about us going away on holiday. What do you think? What do you think about an aeroplane, Gloria?'

Gloria chews her toast. She looks at Mum. Going on an aeroplane is not something that's ever happened before. So she don't know.

'It's noisy,' Mum says. 'It can be. And you can't really wander about. Plus passports are expensive. Might be better off staying in the country, I don't know. What do you reckon? Seaside or something?'

When Gloria was in school some kids go away in the summer, they go to the countries where their families come from or to Spain or to the seaside or Disneyland. They talk about it in school after the summer holidays and Gloria listens and thinks about playing with cousins and going on rides and seeing fish in the sea. Gloria and Mum never go on holiday. But one summer Gloria goes camping with one of the holiday clubs she goes to. They stay in a field outside of London and it's new and exciting. Gloria's never stayed outside of London before. There are no lines on the ground showing where you can't walk, and no red or green lights telling you when to stop and when to go. Just grass and trees and sky. When it rains the ground gets so muddy and wet you could sink right into it and get buried. At night the stars are so bright in the sky, and the clouds rush in front of the moon, twisting into hills and mountains and breaking apart again and moving on. The tents are so thin that it feels like being outside all the time. You only have to undo a zip and there you are, outdoors. When it rains in the night the raindrops tap-tap-tap on the tent right next to her head.

Animals live there. Outside in the wild, not in cages. No one feeds them or looks after them. Anything could happen. Gloria sees them, rabbits in the bushes and deer in the forest, living out in the grass and the trees with no fences and no roads.

One day Gloria finds a rabbit with its head off. It looks like a normal rabbit, grey and fluffy, stretched out slim on its side like it is halfway through running. But it has a red gory mess where its neck should be. And it ends there. There is no head.

Gloria sits and looks at the rabbit for a long time. She thinks about how it would feel to have your head bitten off. How it would hurt. The pain and pain of it, sawing and sawing. No one to stop it. How it would be to die there in a field, in the fresh air and bright sunshine. With no one watching you or controlling you or stopping you from taking risks. How fast you will run from the fox when you know there is no one to call.

Staff come looking for her, shouting 'Gloria!' through the woods. Gloria stands up and goes towards them, leaving the rabbit behind. She don't want them to find her next to it. It feels like she's been doing something bad even though she's just been looking.

Gloria smiles at Mum because she wants to go on holiday. Mum smiles back.

'I know we ain't done it before,' Mum says, 'but I don't see no reason we can't. I'm earning a bit more now and we've had a tough time the last couple of years ain't we. We could both do with a break.'

5

It's been sunny for a lot of days. The park is open longer because it gets dark later. Gloria's not wearing a coat, it's too warm. Inside the pocket of her hoody is Tariq's key. She sits on her bench and looks at their house.

Everyone has gone out of the house and Gloria don't follow them now because Tariq said to stop. But she still watches. She likes seeing them too much. Mum's at work so it ain't a weekend. Tariq will be at college and Sumera and Salim are at school.

Gloria gets up and walks to the park gate. There is sunlight on the ground and it makes little blades of grass shine bright green. Outside the park the tarmac is a purple-pink colour, nice to scrape shoes on, it makes a good sound. There are no cars coming. She crosses the road to the family's house. Here the pavement is slabs of cracked grey cement. It makes a dry chalky sound that Gloria don't like so she don't scrape her shoes.

She goes inside the front garden of the house. It's a narrow space, with a low concrete wall, and there are little shiny stones in the concrete of the wall, brown and blue. There is a green wheely bin and it just fits in between the concrete wall and the house. There are pebbles on the ground and smooth brown tiles leading up to the door. One of the tiles has a diagonal crack and there are little green weeds growing in the crack. The front door is black and shiny. The letter box is silver metal.

Tariq's key is warm from being in her pocket. She puts it into the silver lock. She turns it and it don't move. Maybe it is a key for a different house. She tries again. It still don't move. She turns it the other way, towards the wall, and it moves a little bit, then she turns it back again. She has to do that for her own door sometimes. Yes. This key clicks and turns and she turns it again, her wrist rolling over, and again. And the door opens up.

Inside looks dark. The house smells of air freshener. And then a warmer softer smell hidden underneath. Gloria goes inside. At first it seems dark but then she can see everything. There is a grey carpet on the floor. There are stairs. The walls are white. There is a picture of red and white flowers. There is a long black scuff mark along the wall. There is a wooden door that is half open. Gloria goes in. It is the living room. The TV sits on a yellow wooden cupboard. There is a clock over it, silver with gold lines instead of numbers. There is a grey sofa and a grey armchair. There is a white computer on a desk in a corner of the room. There is a table. Over the table there is a big photo of the family. In the photo the children are younger than now, the boys are not tall and Salim don't have a moustache. The children stand around Mr Miah and the mum. The mum is smiling. Mr Miah is smiling too. He's wearing a white shirt. Sumera is little, she has her hair in bunches and she is wearing a pink dress.

On the table there is a blue-green folder and a pink exercise book and a stack of books and some pens and a watch. The watch is light blue with a light blue clear plastic strap. It has buttons on the side. The time is written in numbers. 11:02. The number 2 flicks and changes to a 3 as Gloria looks. She holds the watch up to her face and looks through the strap. The world turns blurry blue. She puts it down again and looks around. The ceiling in this room is higher than in her house. The house feels open and clean. There is a light coming out of the ceiling with three light bulbs attached to it, like an upside-down tree. Mr Miah lived here. Mr Miah probably sits on this sofa, watching TV. She feels calm inside. Now she don't think of Mr Miah dying on the pavement with all his blood all around him. She thinks of him sitting on the sofa holding a cup of tea and smiling. She looks at the window. The net curtains are thick white but she can see the park through them. The boy on the bike turning round in circles. The bench where she likes to sit.

She goes back through the wooden door and down the corridor. There is the kitchen. Inside the kitchen is normal things. An oven, a sink, cupboards and drawers. The cupboards are red-brown wood. The floor is yellow lino with a pattern of grey lines over it to make it look like tiles. Through the windows is a garden. The garden has grass, and bushes around the edge, and brown wooden fences. There is a bike leaning on the fence. It has red paint on and it is rusty. She goes back to the corridor.

The stairs have grey carpet the same as the hall. She goes up them, holding onto the white painted banister. The paint is shiny, with dips and cracks in it. She runs her thumbnail over them and her nail bounces up and down and it don't catch because the paint is so smooth. At the top of the stairs it's dark. There are three wooden doors. She opens the first one. It's a bathroom. The walls are painted dark grey. There is a bit of black mould on the windowsill. There are lots of bottles of soap and shampoo all on the side of the bath. The bath is white. The toilet is white with a reddy-brown wooden seat. There is a blue pot next to the toilet. There is a yellow mat on the floor. There are towels hanging up, lilac and light blue.

The next door is a small room. There's a bed with a faded My Little Pony duvet cover, pink and yellow, the pink faded to light orange. The door only opens part way because there is a rail behind it crammed with clothes. There are shiny glossy fabrics of gold and pink and green peeking out among the dark trousers and hoodies. The walls are white. There is a chest of drawers wedged between the window and the bed. The top of the drawers has schoolbooks and make-up and a pot of pens. There are shelves over the drawers with more books and pens and CDs. There are photos stuck to the walls of Sumera with Mr Miah and Sumera with all different girls wearing the same black uniform, and then in some photos the girls are wearing bright colours, yellow and gold and blue. Gloria sits on the bed. It's soft. It smells of perfume and the smell sticks in Gloria's throat and makes it ache. The make-up on the chest of drawers is all shiny, golden and silver round boxes and gleaming black square sticks. Like on Mum's dresser. She wants to run her hands over it all and feel all the packs and pots click and slide against each other. Opposite her, under the rack of clothes, is a white plastic bin. Something gold glints inside it. Inside the bin there are old tissues and torn-up bits of paper. There is a gold lid shining through them. She reaches it out. It is an empty lipstick tube. The gold lid is so shiny Gloria can see her own lips and her own eyes reflected in it. She smiles and sees her lips smile in gold. She opens it to make sure. It's empty. She closes it again. It makes a satisfying snap. It's not stealing if it's rubbish anyway, if it was going in the bin. It will be nice in her box. Gold next to the silver key, next to the yellow plastic lighter. She sits on the bed for longer, looking at the gold square tube, clicking it open and shut. Then she puts it in her pocket.

The next room is bigger. There are bunk beds. There are clothes draped over a chair. There is a desk by the window with books and folders piled on it. The room smells of feet and sweat. The curtains are closed. They are black curtains but the light still comes through them a little bit. There is wallpaper that looks blue but it's hard to be sure because it's too dark to tell properly. Gloria stands in the doorway of the room. She thinks of opening the curtains.

There's a noise downstairs. A sudden clunk and thud. The front door.

She jerks with shock and her heart beats fast. Everybody's out. If someone comes home and she is here they might be cross. She stands still and don't breathe. She listens.

There's nothing. No more noise. No footsteps. Maybe someone is standing still downstairs. Maybe it's Tariq. When he sees her he will say It's you innit. I knew it was you. Then he'll say You got to stop following us. He'll look at her again. Like he did in the park. The same park where she went with Jack.

She steps backwards out of the bedroom, one step backwards. She don't trip or fall. She turns around and walks forwards. She walks along to the top of the steps. She walks quiet on the grey carpet like when she plays hide-and-seek when she's a kid. Maybe Tariq's there listening, trying to find her. She goes to the top of the stairs.

The hall looks light, sunshine coming through the semi-circle window at the top of the front door.

She steps on the first step. She don't make a noise. She holds on the banister so she can go slowly and quietly. She holds on tight. Next foot on the next step. And the next one. She keeps looking in the hall.

There is a parcel on the floor. It weren't there before. It must have come through the letterbox and made the noise. Tariq is not here looking for her. None of them are here. But she's feeling frightened now, her heart going too fast. So she goes to the front door and lets herself out. She closes the door tight behind her, like she has to at home. She goes through the park and back towards Green Street, the lipstick and the key clicking together in her pocket.

6

Gloria and Mum get the train to Margate. In Margate it's sunny. By the sea everything is blue and big and open. It makes her breathe slower. They stay in a flat near the sea. The flat is smaller than their house, it has one room with a big bed, and one room with a sofa and a kitchen inside the same room, and a bathroom. Gloria sleeps in the bed and Mum pulls out the sofa and makes a bed on that. The flat is up two flights of stairs, like Jack's was. The flat has a balcony with two chairs that they sit on in the evenings and look at the sea. The sea makes a rhythm, over and over, small soft crashes. Gloria likes it. When she sits and listens to the sea she don't play no words in her head. She just hears the waves. The sea is blue-green, like in pictures, like her box and her favourite mug. On the beach is yellow-brown sand, not stones. They sit on the balcony in the evening and the sky goes all orange and purple as the sun goes down. Mum drinks wine. Gloria has some too. The wine is yellow and sour and when she drinks enough of it, it makes her feel safe.

In the daytime they sit on the beach. Mum brings towels. She has a green towel and Gloria has a red-and-white striped one. They put the towels on the sand and lay on the towels. Mum puts sun cream on Gloria so she don't burn. 'Do me back Glor,' she says. Gloria rubs the sun cream on Mum's back, over the little brown spots on her skin. Mum reads her book or lays with her eyes closed like she's asleep. Gloria sits and looks at the sea and looks at shells she finds in the sand and looks at the people. There's lots of white people in Margate. There is a man on the beach who is bright red from the sun. It looks like he is covered in blood. Gloria don't like looking at him. She gets up and walks to the sea and walks inside it. It's very very cold and it's clear and bright, the sunlight making lots of flashes on its surface, and she can see her own feet and legs inside the water. The waves rush up and make the sea come up higher, cold to her knees. The sand turns to brown mud in the waves then sinks back to sand again. She sits down and lets the water chill her up to her waist, lets it splash in her face and make the light dazzle her eyes. She's wearing her red bikini so it's okay if she gets wet. The sea rushes around her hands and wrists, it covers her legs. When she gets too cold she gets out again and goes back to Mum. The sand sticks to her. It sticks to the sun cream. It sticks to Mum too. Even when they lay on the towels the sand still gets all over them. It stays on their skin and clothes and shoes. It gets on the floor in the holiday flat. When it's time to go home, Mum tries to sweep it out onto the balcony, but there's still tiny grains everywhere. Back in London Gloria finds it in her hair, in her bag, and in the pockets of her shorts, even after a long time.

Mum goes to work again. Gloria walks around more. She goes to her bench in the family's park. The grass in the park is all dry and brown. The park is open till late because it's light for a long time. She stays there and sees them all get home. Sumera gets home first. Then the mum gets home, the faded woman. She comes home when it's still light, not like in winter. She is wearing a dark-green headscarf and a long dark-green dress. Then Salim gets home and last of all Tariq. He is wearing black jeans and a blue T-shirt.

The aqua glow of the TV comes through the white net curtains, shining the same colour as the sea. Gloria remembers the fresh cold water rushing on her ankles, pulling her, the sand disappearing from under her feet like the world is falling away. Part of the sky is orange. Part of it is pink. It is getting dark.

She gets up and leaves the park. She walks past the railings, the other side of the street from the family's house. The windows of the house are shining pink in the sunset. The house looks beautiful. She thinks of the rooms inside, the lamp sprouting from the ceiling like a tree, the grey sofa and the picture of red flowers in the hall. Shadows move through the curtains. A figure coming close. The net curtain lifts up and she sees Salim and the TV behind him with a man's face on the screen. Salim opens the window at the top. He drops the net curtain back down and disappears. She hears a girl's laugh and a boy's shout floating out from the open window across the road towards her. She sees Mr Miah on the ground beside Jack's bare feet and shakes her head, closes her eyes to try and make the picture go away. Over her head a street light comes on. Orange light. A dull shine on the pavement.

Gloria crosses the road to the house. Mr Miah said Do you want a lift love? Maybe he would drive her to his house and take her inside, let her sit on the sofa. Give her a cup of tea. She wants to go inside. She wants to go inside and be with them all, laughing and shouting, feeling too hot, feeling the sofa against her legs.

She crosses the road to the house. The voices get clearer.

'Shut up Suto bhaiya, you're such a prick man,' Sumera is saying, but she's laughing with the words.

Gloria goes towards the black front door. The brown tiles are smooth and slippery under her feet. She slides her feet along them, without stepping. She finds the round silver of the key in her pocket. She puts the key inside the lock. It won't turn. She remembers the trick she did before. She jiggles it and twists it and it works. It only turns once.

The door opens. Inside is all warm bright light. There is a bug flying around the light in the hall, casting jolting shadows. The voices and the laughter stop. No one is talking no more. She steps along the hall and pushes on the wooden door into the living room.

The door opens.

Everyone is staring at her. Salim and Tariq and Sumera. Tariq and Sumera are standing up and Salim is on the armchair, half sitting, half standing. He screams when he sees Gloria and his voice cracks, a sharp creaking noise. Sumera's mouth is slightly open. Her scarf is not there and her hair is long, down to her waist. Tariq is staring and staring.

'It's you,' Tariq says, 'Oh my god it's you.'

Sumera screams, 'Amma, Amma!'

'Get out,' Salim says, standing up. 'Get out!'

'I thought it was Abbu,' Tariq says. 'I thought it was Abbu coming home.' He puts his head in his hands and cries. He sobs loud, like a small child. Then he stops quickly. He wipes his eyes. 'The way you screamed man,' he says to Salim, his voice shaking, but laughing too. He laughs again and it sounds like sobbing.

'Shut up,' Salim says.

Tariq stops laughing. He wipes his hands over his face hard. He comes towards Gloria. 'Get out,' he says.

Gloria hears someone behind her. She turns round. The faded woman is there. Her hair is loose, down to her shoulders. She looks different without her scarf. She's wearing a thin black dress. Her mouth is open. She touches Gloria's arm. Her hand feels cool. 'Get out,' she says. 'Get out of my house. Get away from my children.'

She pushes on Gloria's arm. Gloria moves a step backwards and another until she is standing in the hall. The woman stands in the doorway so Gloria can't get in the living room. Tariq comes and stands beside her. He is taller than her. He wipes his eyes. 'How did you get in?' he says to Gloria.

'One of you must have left the door open,' says the mum. Sumera and Salim are behind her, watching Gloria with wide eyes. 'You need to go,' the woman says to Gloria. 'You need to go now before I call the police.' Her voice shakes. She sounds frightened.

Gloria smiles, to show that she wants them all to be happy, that she don't want to scare them.

'Don't laugh. Don't you dare laugh,' the woman shouts.

'Get out,' Tariq says. 'You know what? Sumera, Salim. Call the police. Call them now.'

Sumera and Salim move behind him.

'Police, please,' she hears Salim say.

Gloria turns around. She goes to the door and opens it and steps outside into the evening. The air smells salty and sweet. A motorbike roars past. There is a dog barking, over the other side of the park. Gloria is crying. She walks down the street crying and crying but she don't make no noise. Tears keep coming down her face. She bites on the side of her hand, hard. In her pocket she clenches her fist around the silver key, feels the jagged edge of it press into her skin like her palm will burst open.

The next day a police comes round to her house. She talks to Mum and she talks to Gloria. She says Gloria can't see Mr Miah's family no more, she can't go outside their house and she must never go inside their house again under any circumstances. Do you understand? The family don't like it. It's very hard and very upsetting for them. They need space and everybody needs to move on.

2017

1

Mirror.

The thing is behind her face.

She must have had a bad dream or a remembering dream. Because the thing is there today proper, sitting on her heavy. She looks in the mirror and sticks her tongue out, bares her teeth like a monster, rrroarrr! She looks into her own eyes. She leans her forehead against her own forehead on the glass.

When she comes out the bathroom she sees Sam in the hallway, at the bottom of the stairs.

'Alright Gloria?' Sam calls, looking up.

'Morning,' Gloria says.

Sam goes into the office. Gloria goes downstairs. She's still wearing her black jogging bottoms and T-shirt that she wears for sleep. She rubs at her eyes where they feel all crusty and itchy.

Downstairs, Rose is sitting at the table eating a bowl of cereal. Tyrone is in the kitchen. Sam and Tyrone are working this morning. Sharifah will be in later. Staff are important to know because they come and go, and different staff give you different kinds of days. The other residents are important too, but they are always the same. Gloria likes Suzanne and Haider and Blessing, she tolerates Rose, she don't mind Sonam.

'Morning Gloria,' Tyrone calls. 'Do you want a cup of tea?'

Gloria pauses, thinking, then she says, 'Yeah.' She shoots the word out. She pulls out a chair and sits down opposite Rose.

'Morning Rose,' she says.

'Morning.'

Rose is crunching her cereal, eating with her mouth open so Gloria can see her tongue coated white from the milk, and mashed up bits of cornflake moving around between her teeth. Gloria hates the noise of it. Pops and squidges. It makes her think of all the food in Rose's mouth and Rose's tongue and teeth and the food going down Rose's throat and her windpipe and all of this inside the skin of her neck and how someone could put her hands round it and squeeze, and Rose's throat would curl up and get tight. Gloria kicks at the table leg with her foot and hums to block out the noise. Tyrone brings her the tea. 'Close your mouth Rose,' he says, 'we don't all need a view of your breakfast.'

Rose laughs and mumbles, 'Sorry.'

Gloria tries slurping her tea to make the sound of Rose eating go away, but it don't work. She picks up her tea carefully and walks to the window. A little bit splashes hot on her fingers. She stands by the window and drinks the tea looking out at the park. Tyrone has the radio on, and she tries to make her ears think about the song playing and not Rose's eating. She follows the song with her mind, following the words up and down. She watches the trees, and the boys gathering on the benches and kicking a football around on the grass. She likes it that her house is beside the park. The house garden is just yellow paving stones but there is a gate in the garden wall that leads right into the park.

Gloria's been living at Greengate Lodge a long time. Before she lives there, she lives with her mum. But her mum talks to her about it a lot and says, 'I wanna see you get settled somewhere Gloria, while I can still make sure it's a decent place. So you can get settled bit by bit and you can come and see me whenever you like, does that make sense darling?'

Her mum looks for places Gloria could live, and they go to visit them together and Mum talks to staff. Mum argues on the phone with the bloody council a lot. For a long time they're looking at houses and her mum is arguing on the phone with the bloody council in the evenings. Then Gloria moves to Greengate Lodge. She likes it because of the park.

'Perfect for you, eh, Gloria?' Mum says. 'And nice and close by. Only take about fifteen minutes to walk it.'

Mum hugs Gloria and cries when it's time for her to move in, and Gloria cries too. But that is a long time ago. Now it's okay and she don't cry about it no more.

Tyrone comes to stand beside her, holding his own mug of tea. 'You'll like this one Gloria,' he says. 'I tell you what I was thinking about the other day. I was thinking, what if we're all in a video game. Imagine that, yeah. And me and you are just like programmed characters. In the background. The way you act is only cos you been programmed that way. Same with me. We just doing our lives, same routine over and over, just following the programming. And then I thought what about if – you know them geezers who hurt people, who do mad shit. Sorry for swearing, but them geezers on the news driving cars into people and that. Or blowing people up. Maybe they're the players. The real people plugged into the game. Holding the controls. Just driving cars into people, walking round killing people and that. People who ain't got nothing to lose and they just wanna hurt people, think it's funny to hurt people. Maybe they're the real people playing the game, and they know we're just lines of computer code or something mad like that so it don't matter if they kill us. Know what I mean? And maybe when they go to prison or die or whatever, that's just them logging out.' He nudges her. 'What do you think?'

She flinches.

Tyrone looks at her. 'Gloria? You okay?' he says, putting his hand up to touch her shoulder but stopping short.

She don't answer him. She stares out at the park. She starts humming. Rose's eating noise and all of Tyrone's words, she wants to cover them up. She runs her tongue inside her own hot mouth to know it's empty.

'Well,' he says. 'I was only messing, it was just a thought and that, you know what I'm saying. You know I like talking to you.'

Gloria goes in the park. The park is better than being stuck indoors all day like Haider. Haider don't like to go out. When Abdi's on he takes Haider down the shops or away on the bus. Haider don't mind the trips but he don't ever ask for them. Once a week he walks down the road to Iceland for his shopping. That's it. Gloria don't care either way, Haider can do what he likes. She likes being outdoors as long as it ain't raining.

Trees are good, trees are good. She sings the words like a song in her head. It sounds like a song she used to hear on the radio a long time ago. Yellow leaves are falling off the trees. There are still a few flowers in the ground, poking up from the earth. Gloria walks on the concrete paths, not on the grass. She don't stop when she goes past the boys on the benches. They are men really. Fully grown. But they look like boys. They have left her alone every other day, so they will most likely leave her alone today. They talk quietly to each other, muttering words out the side of their mouths, like they're scared of being caught talking. Yo bruv what you sayin you all good. Where's Derrick at. Fist to fist. A mild autumn breeze blows their words away as she walks past them.

It's the fifth of November. Gloria knows because after breakfast Sam says, 'Don't forget, we're going fireworks tonight, everyone. We leave here at half five. Okay? If you want to eat your dinner before we go, make sure you have it in plenty of time. Don't be coming here for half five saying you still need to use the loo or find your bus pass or whatever. Ready to go by half five. Got it? Blessing, got it?'

Blessing nods.

'Suzanne? Sonam? Gloria? Haider?'

They nod and smile, because the tone of her voice is joking a bit.

'Everyone remember,' Sam says. 'Remember remember the fifth of November.'

Gloria looks at the climbing frame to her side, blue paint flaking off and showing brown metal. There's a small girl making her way up its lower rungs, her tongue stuck out in concentration. The girl is bundled into a green jacket which is too fat and thick for her to move her arms properly. A woman stands beside the climbing frame, watching.

There is a big puddle, like a lake, with leaves curled at its edge. The water is dark like in the fountain. Who knows how deep it goes? Maybe it will go all the way to her waist if she steps in it. Or even over her head. Maybe she'll drown. She walks round the edge of the puddle, on the grass. The grass is all muddy and squishy, her trainers slipping. She steps carefully, because one of her trainers has a crack in the bottom and it will let the water in. Gloria's mum complains when Gloria has broken shoes or rips in her coat, she says the staff in Gloria's house are useless and how comes no one's taken her to buy new things? You can't walk around like that Gloria, you look a mess. But Gloria likes the staff anyway. She heard Sharifah complaining about her mum once too, after her mum went home. Sharifah's talking to Sam in the office, saying, That woman's never satisfied. If she knows it needs doing, why don't she do it? By the time she's told us, she might as well have done it herself. She sees Gloria listening and gets up and closes the office door.

Gloria goes to the fountain. There are two men sitting on one of the benches. They are talking to each other in a different language. They are drinking from cans. Gloria goes to the other side. The fountain is like a giant concrete dish, with black water in and railings all round it. There is one day she came to the fountain and it was all cleaned up. Orange fish swim in the black water, their scales glinting in the sunlight. Lilies float on the water, and lily pads. Gloria never pays much attention to the fountain before that, but she starts coming every day, watching the bright bodies of the fish twisting through the water. Looking at the flowers and the clear spray catching the light. Then people start throwing rubbish in. Old bottles and crisp packets. The water stops running and the fountain gets covered in green slime and it goes back to how it was. Sometimes she thinks she sees the fish still, just a flash of gold, a movement in the dark water.

A woman comes to sit with the two men. It is the woman who knows Jack and says hello to Gloria. The woman is carrying a blue carrier bag and she takes a can out of it and starts drinking. She is skinny with brown hair down to her shoulders. She is wearing a dark-green jacket and a dark-red scarf. She waves at Gloria but she don't smile. The woman looks very old and very thin. She smells bad so Gloria don't go close to her a lot. The woman sits with the men and they talk in English. They laugh. Gloria leans on the fence around the fountain and looks into the dark water. There's a plastic bottle floating, hazy and dull. She tries to see a gold fish but nothing moves.

'Hey,' the woman says to her. 'Oi darling.'

Gloria looks at her. The woman's eyes are little bright dots. Gloria looks back at the pond again.

'I see your fella the other day,' the woman says.

The railings are rough under Gloria's hands, the paint flaking off them. They are cold. They make her hands ache.

'That Jack,' the woman says. 'I'm sure it was him. He said hello to me. He must of got out. You seen him?'

Gloria keeps looking at the black water.

'Ain't he come to say hello?' the woman says. She laughs and the men laugh too.

Gloria's chest is tight. She turns and walks away from the woman and the men and the fountain. She can hear them laughing behind her.

She goes on the path. Boys are playing football in the middle of the grass wearing shorts and T-shirts. There is a man shouting at them. Come on, come on, keep it moving! Good! The boys' breath comes out in little puffs and huffs of steam, like they're smoking.

Gloria can't take a proper deep breath in. The air is not real air, it's made of something that won't move, won't be sucked in and out. She has to take small small breaths, just filling the top of her chest. There are two girls sitting on the swings, slicing back and forth through the air, calling across to each other. Did you see Madison on Friday? Yeah. You know she's moving over Dagenham? They are pointing their toes and arcing their whole bodies to make the swings go faster and higher. An old lady sits on the bench with her shopping trolley. It is the bench where Gloria and Jack sit together. The lady nods and smiles at Gloria because they see each other in the park a lot. Gloria don't smile back because of her chest being so tight and having to take small breaths. On the next bench a man sits sucking on a little machine, blowing out lots and lots of smoke. There is a big cloud of his smoke over the path. It smells like strawberry bubblegum. Above her the trees rustle and sigh in the breeze. A carrier bag caught in branches rattles and rattles, a hard noise thudding in Gloria's head. She tries to listen to it. It catches the words the woman said and rattles them against her ears.

That Jack That Jack That Jack. He must of got out.

Gloria ain't seen him. She looks every day. She comes to this park every day because she lives beside it and she don't see Jack. She feels so full inside, something hot running through her from her chest down through her hands and feet. Your fella, the woman says.

2

It's lunchtime but Gloria don't want to go home. Rose and Blessing will eat loudly and people will argue about using the kitchen and she only has pasta anyway. Her cupboard is full of pasta sachets, because they were doing a special offer in the supermarket so she bought a lot. They are easy to cook, just a mug and kettle. Gloria you can't have pasta for breakfast, Mum says, but Mum don't live with her, and Tyrone or the others might tell her she can't have pasta for breakfast but they won't say it like they expect her to take any notice.

She walks out of the park. Buses go past. She goes past the Greenway and down past the leisure centre where the air smells of chlorine. It's 2017. The calendar in the living room has the year on it. So it has been a long long time Jack has been in prison for. Lots of years.

There is a man walking towards her. He is wearing a faded orange hoody with the hood pulled up over his head, sitting low across his face. She can't see his face. His hands are in his pockets so she can't see his hands. He comes right close up towards her. She is staring and staring at him. She steps into where he is walking so she can see under his hood and see his face. He stops short.

'Alright love,' he says, 'what you doing?' He pushes his eyebrows up. He looks surprised. Gloria can see he ain't Jack. He's the wrong colour, with dark hair and a beard, brown eyes.

Gloria steps away from him. She puts her hands in her pockets. The man keeps walking. He looks back at her and shakes his head. Gloria is breathing fast. There's a feeling in her chest like she needs to split open and let herself out. Inside her pockets she squeezes her furry blue purse and her phone. Coins move and shift inside her purse. She presses the buttons of her phone and makes them click. Her mum bought her the phone. It is small and black with silver buttons. Gloria don't use it lots. It has Mum's number stored in it, and the number for Greengate Lodge where she lives, and the staff mobile phone number. Whoever answers the staff phone depends on who is working and who is holding the phone that day. She gets the phone out of her pocket. She looks at the phone and presses to make it work. She presses the down arrow button until she finds the word Mum, then she presses the green-phone button. Call. There is ringing, brr-brr, brr-brr.

Mum don't answer. Gloria waits, holding the phone pressed tight against her ear so she can hear clearly. It rings and rings. Then a machine voice says, 'Hello…Can't take your call at the moment. Please leave a message after the tone.'

Gloria waits. She don't speak. She thinks about what to say. 'Hello,' she starts. Then she says, 'Gloria,' so her mum will know who it is. Before she can say anything else there is a long beeping sound, and the phone is quiet again. She looks at the screen and it shows a phone hanging up, then the light fades. Gloria puts the phone back in her pocket.

On Barking Road there's a little patch of grass inside a low wall. There are people sitting on the wall drinking from cans. She looks to see if Jack is there. But he's not there. She crosses the road to the bus stop.

The bus she wants comes. It's low with no upstairs. She steps inside the red doors, touches her blue rectangle pass on the yellow circle. She sits down near the front.

She watches out the window. Shops go past. Houses are crammed together, curling away into different streets. The trees have been cut all the way up so they are thick brown trunks with blobs of green at the top, like the trees she draws.

The bus turns a corner and goes up one of the side streets. She hears the bell go, tnng, and she waits in her seat, not moving. It reaches her stop. She thinks about staying on the bus, going all the way up to Stratford, to the big grey steps and the loud bright shopping centre.

But she stands up. She walks to the doors, holding onto the bar so she won't fall over. A lady is getting off the bus with a pushchair. There is a baby in the pushchair. The baby looks up at the sky as the chair is tipped back. The baby's face is still. The mum takes care, watching where her feet are treading then watching where she puts the buggy, straining to lift its back wheels. The clear plastic buggy cover is folded back and bunched up. It catches the light in jagged shards, like pieces of mirror. Gloria watches the baby's face and the light splintering on the plastic. Then it's her turn to get off the bus. There is a feeling of motion when she is standing on the bus, the engine thrumming beneath her feet. She steps onto the red tarmac and the motion is gone. The ground is hard beneath her feet. She scrapes her shoe on the tarmac to hear the scraping noise and feel the dips and bumps.

The woman rights the buggy and walks away.

Gloria turns around and goes in the opposite direction.

It was a long time ago the last time she walked on this street. One of the houses is new. The old house that was there before must have been knocked down. The new one is made of yellow bricks with bright white plastic window frames.

Gloria gets to the patch of scrubby grass. The twisted metal railing and the broken concrete posts have gone. She stands. Her foot is on a paving stone that is cracked and bowed in the middle. The sole of her shoe folds and bends into the crack. The black tarmac and white markings of the road are faded to different shades of grey. A car goes past. She closes her eyes. She opens them again and looks at the winter sky.

She breathes hard, trying to make the air work properly and go in and out. She feels sick.

That Jack. I'm sure it was him. He said hello to me. You seen him?

Gloria looks across the road at the house opposite. The dark wood door with no windows. The dull metal letterbox halfway down. The small shut-down closed-in appearance.

She looks up at the high window. She can't see in. She still partly expects to see him come leaning out the window, smoking a fag. Look up and down the street, checking for trouble. See her and call out Gloria! She looks up where he would be, ready to smile. But the smile catches on her lips, won't form. She stands and watches and she wonders who is in that room now and what they are doing and what they are saying. Maybe he's come back. Maybe he's here. Maybe he's close by, watching her.

She looks over her shoulder. She sees the empty grass, the houses with shrouded windows and solid doors. She can hear traffic on the main road, at the end of the street. Sirens speeding past and disappearing. She turns back to Jack's window again. She stands and looks for a long time. He ain't here. She waits and watches to see if something will happen. If somebody will call out her name.

Then she turns away from his window. Her foot straightens as it lifts from the broken paving stone. She walks away. She don't look across at the other side of the road, just in case there is still blood. Pictures are pushing at the edge of her, trying to get in. She keeps walking down towards the main road, where the fruit and veg stalls spill out onto the pavements and the people walk up and down and the buses rattle past and the sirens scream.

She can see Canary Wharf in the distance with other big glass towers next to it. She can see the supermarket and the flyover, and all the new flats, brightly coloured and gleaming, all the way up into the sky. When Jack lived here there was a factory over the other side of the station. It made food. Most mornings the fumes make the air smell bad, thick like rotten pasta and old milk. Now the factory is gone. The street market across the road has gone too. Now it's a smooth concrete space.

She goes to the bus stop to wait for her bus home. In her pocket her phone starts buzzing. It don't make a ringing noise. Staff said she should have it on silent so people don't rob her. She takes the phone out and looks at it, the screen flashing blue-white light. She presses the green-phone button to answer.

'Gloria?' says Mum's voice.

Gloria don't speak.

'Gloria, answer me, for Christ's sake,' Mum says. 'I'm on the phone, remember?'

'Hello,' Gloria says, which is what to say when you answer the phone.

'Hello,' Mum says. 'Are you okay?'

Gloria waits, then she remembers that she has to speak or Mum won't know. 'Yes,' she says.

'So what's up?' Mum says. 'You called me earlier, and you

never use your phone if you can help it. Has something happened?'

Gloria don't speak.

'Should I be worried?' Mum says.

'No,' Gloria says, because she knows she shouldn't cause Mum any worry.

'Has someone robbed you? Took something?'

Gloria shakes her head.

'Gloria? Answer me.'

'No.'

'Do you wanna come round?' Mum says. 'You know you can come over any time. Just call me first innit, check I'm in. Come over now if you like. I'll put the kettle on.'

'No,' says Gloria. 'Fireworks.' She went to her mum's on Friday night. She might go again tomorrow.

'Oh, you going fireworks tonight?' Mum says.

'Yeah,' says Gloria.

'With your friends from home? The staff going?'

'Yeah,' says Gloria.

'Well have a good time,' Mum says. 'Might go up there myself later on.'

Gloria don't speak.

'If I do I'll call you.'

Gloria waits.

'Well, are you okay?' Mum says.

'Yeah.'

'Okay. Are you home? Where are you? It sounds like you're outside.'

'Yeah. Going home now.'

'You getting the bus?'

'Yeah.'

'Okay. I'm gonna call your house, okay? Get them to check if everything's alright. I'm gonna tell them you're on your way home, so make sure you get there. I don't wanna be worrying about you, you hear me?'

'Yeah.'

'Alright. See you later Gloria. Love you.'

Gloria pauses. Then she says, 'I love you. Bye.'

3

When Gloria gets inside the front door, Sharifah comes out the office. 'Gloria, I've just had your mum on the phone,' she says. 'Are you okay?'

Gloria don't say nothing.

'Has something happened?' Sharifah says gently.

Gloria takes off her coat and hangs it up.

'Your mum said you called her,' Sharifah says. 'Was something the matter?'

Gloria don't speak.

'If you don't say nothing I can't help you,' Sharifah says. Her voice is calm.

Gloria shakes her head. 'Nothing,' she says.

'You sure?' Sharifah says. 'Has anyone talked to you, or tried to take something off you?'

People have tried to take stuff off Gloria before. One

time a man comes up to her and says Can I have some money? It's on a street with no one else around. And when Gloria walks past him he pushes her and grabs her by her coat and says, I said give me your fucking money. His teeth are gritted and his eyes are squinting at her all angry and hard. A bit of his spit flies out and lands on her face. Gloria gives him some money and he runs away from her. Another time she is walking with her shiny red handbag that she got in East Ham market. It's made of shiny plastic and she likes the way the light cracks on its surface when it bends. And a man walks past and pulls the bag really hard so Gloria lets go, and the man runs away with it. It is on the main road. People chase him but he gets away. So now Gloria tries to stay on busier streets only and she don't carry things in a handbag no more.

Sharifah looks at her like she's thinking hard. Her arms are folded.

Gloria walks past her. She needs to get dinner because of going out.

'Gloria!' Sharifah says. 'Come back please, I'm still talking to you.'

Gloria turns around but she don't go back.

Sharifah looks at her for a bit. 'If anything happens, or if anything's worrying you, talk to one of us, okay?' she says eventually. 'That's what we're here for.'

Gloria don't say nothing.

'Okay?' Sharifah says.

Gloria nods.

'Good,' Sharifah says. 'Okay. You can go now, Gloria. Thank you for talking to me.'

Gloria goes into the main room. Everybody is there to make dinner because of going out tonight. Sonam is standing to one side flicking her fingers back and forth in front of her face, making it so the day flashes on and off. Blessing is sitting at the table. Rose is walking around the table, pulling all the chairs out and then pushing them in again, trying to decide where to sit. Suzanne is sitting on the sofa drinking from a mug, but her attention is on the kitchen. Sam and Tyrone are in the kitchen making cups of tea. The door is open.

Gloria stands near the kitchen and looks in at Tyrone and Sam. She can hear them talking.

'I got some more of that good stuff,' Tyrone says. 'If you still want some.'

'Yeah, I'll have some,' Sam says. She don't look at him. She takes the teabags out of three steaming mugs.

'You can come round again when we get off work, if you like,' Tyrone says.

'Maybe,' Sam says. Gloria sees her smiling. She is not looking at him.

'You ain't worried about last time are you?' Tyrone says. 'Look, last time was nice. You could of stayed. I'd make you breakfast.'

Worrieda bout.

The kettle boils.

Sam looks at Tyrone and he raises his eyebrows at her. 'I'm not—' he says, 'I mean I ain't trying— Look.'

Sam smiles again, warm and pleased. Tyrone smiles back at her. They are looking at each other and smiling. Then Gloria thinks maybe Sam and Tyrone are a couple. Maybe Sam and Tyrone are in love. Maybe they walk around together holding hands. They sleep next to each other at night. They have sex. They give presents on Valentine's Day. She remembers walking round the park with Jack and how it felt to have somebody really want to see her.

'Later,' Sam says. 'Talk about it later.' She gets the milk out of the fridge and pours it into the teas. She turns round and sees Gloria standing there. 'Gloria,' she says, 'Do you want tea? Tyrone's just doing more.'

'Tea coming up, Gloria,' Tyrone says. He takes the kettle and pours it into three more mugs. He don't look up. He focuses on the kettle and the pouring.

'Can you take these to Rose and Blessing?' Sam says, holding out two of the mugs. 'That's Blessing's, it's got sugar in it,' she adds, nodding at one of them.

Gloria puts her hand out. Sam has to put the mugs down on the side again so she can give Gloria the handles to hold. Gloria takes them over to Rose and Blessing, the china hot against her knuckles.

'Thank you Gloria,' says Rose.

'Yeah, thank you Gloria,' says Blessing.

Gloria goes and stands by the window and looks at the park. The sky is going dark blue, the last group of boys making their way out. The trees are moving in the wind, big and clean. Sam brings out tea for Sonam and Gloria.

Sonam stops flicking her fingers and takes the mug. Sam gives Gloria hers.

There used to be arguments at mealtimes a lot because everybody wanted to get in the kitchen at the same time to make their food. So now the staff make tea for everybody, and they all take turns to make their food, and they drink their tea while they're waiting. And it's a lot more peaceful.

'Right,' Tyrone says, coming out with his own mug of tea. 'Kitchen's free. Who wants it first?'

Gloria don't want to go in the kitchen and get her food ready until Rose has been in and got hers. If she can be cooking her pasta while Rose is eating, then she has to spend less time with Rose's noisy open-mouthed chew. And if Rose is already sitting down eating when Gloria comes out, Gloria can choose a seat far away from her. If Gloria gets her food first, Rose might come and sit next to her to eat and then all the sounds would be really loud in Gloria's ears and do her head in.

Rose stands up and says, 'I'm going first.'

But Tyrone says, 'You're always first, Rose. Let someone else have a turn. Gloria? You wanna get your dinner now?'

Gloria shakes her head.

'You sure?' Tyrone says. 'You don't wanna get in and get your food first? You always wait.'

Gloria shakes her head again.

'Suit yourself,' says Tyrone. 'Blessing?'

'Yeah,' Blessing says. He stands up and goes to the kitchen.

Rose kicks the wall.

'Rose, cool it,' Sam says. 'Remember, these lot need to eat now because we're going out to the fireworks. It'll be your turn soon.'

'I'm going out too,' Rose says.

Haider walks into the room.

'Want a cup of tea, Haider?' says Sam.

'Yes please,' he says.

'I need to get my food,' Rose says.

'Five minutes,' Sam says. 'You can't always go first.' She goes and gets the mug of tea they made for Haider. 'It's a bit cold now,' she tells him.

'Fine,' Haider says, smiling wide. He carries his tea over to the table. 'Got sugar in it?' he says.

'Yeah,' says Sam. 'Two.'

Haider nods and smiles. 'Thanks Sam.'

'I've gotta get my dinner,' Rose says. 'I'm going to the pub. I'm gonna meet a man and have sex.'

'Just be careful,' Sam says.

'Don't tell me what to do,' Rose says. 'I'm not a kid.'

'I'm not telling you what to do,' Sam says. 'It's just advice.'

Blessing comes out of the kitchen with a steaming plate of rice and Rose takes her turn. She comes and sits next to Gloria with her microwave macaroni cheese. Gloria gets up and goes to the kitchen. Tyrone moves aside to let her in. 'Taking your turn now Gloria,' he says. 'You're too polite, you don't always need to let everyone else go first you know.'

Gloria reaches up and opens her cupboard and gets her pasta packet down. She picks up her mug from the draining board. She boils the kettle and waits for it to click off to show it's done. When it's boiled she pours the hot water into her mug and watches the pasta bloom.

Sam comes into the kitchen. 'Gloria, you having pasta again?' she says.

'Pasta for breakfast, lunch and tea,' Tyrone says.

'We'll have to do some cooking lessons with you,' Sam says.

Gloria takes a fork and goes out into the dining room with her food. She sits down at the other end of the table from Rose.

But Rose is eating so loud still.

Gloria hates this sound of the macaroni sticking and squishing inside Rose's mouth. She hates the sound of the food going down Rose's throat, and Rose's tongue working wetly on the pulp of pasta. She puts her hands over her ears. She bites on her tongue but it don't help. She slaps her ears once, hard. She looks at Rose and frowns and screws up her face to look bad at her. She is feeling mad angry. Rose is looking at Gloria, still eating. Gloria feels like Rose is eating to spite her now. Rose frowns back at Gloria.

'Why you looking at me?' Rose yells through a mouthful of food.

Gloria screws up her face at Rose more.

'Stop looking at me Gloria!' Rose yells. Gloria can see all the food going round in her mouth. Gloria hits her hand on the table, open-palmed. She wants the table wood to smack on her hand and hurt it. She wants to feel like she hit Rose.

'Calm down,' Blessing says.

'Be quiet,' Rose says to him.

Sam and Tyrone come out of the kitchen where they were making food for Sonam and Haider.

'What's up?' Tyrone says. And Sam says, 'Rose, why you shouting?'

The others are quiet. Blessing is looking between Rose and Gloria. Suzanne is staring down at her tea.

'Gloria's looking at me,' Rose says. 'Stop looking at me Gloria. I'll hit you!'

Gloria keeps on looking. She imagines Rose hitting her, the feeling of Rose's hand smacking into her face.

'What's your problem? What's your problem with me?' Rose yells. She sounds like she will cry.

'Okay, okay,' Sam says. She goes up to Rose and tries to get in her line of sight but the table is in her way. 'Rose, calm down,' she says. 'You need to stop shouting. Stop shouting.'

'Stop shouting,' Blessing says.

'Alright Blessing,' says Sam.

'Don't tell me to stop shouting,' Rose yells at Blessing.

Tyrone says, 'Rose! Let's go into the other room and talk about it.'

'No, it's her fault! She's a bitch!' Rose yells, pointing at Gloria.

Gloria points back at Rose and pulls a nasty face. She slams her hand on the table and shouts. One short blast of noise. Aaaah! She is angry with Rose. Furious. She can't find the words she wants. She wants Rose to hit her. She wants to hit Rose and dig her fingernails into Rose's skin and rip pieces off of it, feel it soft and warm and bloody on her fingers, sticky. She stands up and pushes her chair back and it falls over. She kicks the table. Everybody's plates jump.

'Gloria!' Sam says, shocked.

Gloria stands with her fists clenched. She screams at Rose. 'Too much noise! Too much noise! Fuck. Too much noise!' She presses her fists to her ears, hard, pressing right in like she might crack her own skull. She likes the pressure of it. She closes her eyes.

Sam comes to stand in front of her. 'Gloria,' she says. 'Calm. You're the one making too much noise now.'

Tears are wet on Gloria's cheeks, her eyes salty and hot. Sam's hand is on her arm. Gloria stands there breathing hard. She is shaking. She feels so bad inside her, she feels sick like the entire world is making her sick and there's nowhere she can go to get better. She keeps pressing in on her own head.

'Come and sit down,' Sam says. 'Come and sit down over there.'

Gloria has her eyes closed still. She feels Sam put her other arm around her. She lets go of her ears and grabs onto Sam's arms.

4

They are all sitting on the bottom deck of the bus because people like Haider find it difficult to go up the stairs. So everybody sits downstairs together. Gloria is sitting closest to the door, next to a lady she don't know. The lady is beside the window but Gloria can still see out the window, all the lights of the shops and cars shining in the dark. Tyrone and Haider are sitting behind Gloria, and Suzanne and Blessing are over on the other side, with Sam and Sonam behind them.

The bus drives slowly up Barking Road. It is full of people. There are families with children getting on at every stop.

'Reckon everyone's going to the fireworks,' Tyrone says, and Sam nods.

The bus goes over the hill by the Greenway. Out the window Gloria sees a girl walking along looking at her phone, the screen lighting up her face and hood cold blue.

The bus stops at the lights and the girl walks faster and turns the corner.

This is the crossing where Gloria first met Jack. Where they see each other on the bench and go to the park. 'Jack,' says Jack inside her mind. He puts his hand out for her to shake. She closes her eyes and bites the side of her tongue and presses her hands tight against her head to feel where she is and where she ends and where her outlines are.

He must of got out. You seen him?

'When is it?' Gloria says to Sam, across the aisle. Because she can't feel what time it is inside her. It could be any time. Any year, any day. She can't tell.

'When is it?' Sam echoes. 'What time does it start, you mean? You worried about being late? Fireworks start at seven. We got plenty of time, Gloria.'

'It's winter,' Gloria says.

'Yeah. Autumn, winter. It's November. November the fifth, remember? That's why we're going fireworks. It's bonfire night.'

Bomb fire.

Bomb fire night.

'We're going to see the fireworks,' Blessing calls across. 'We're going Wanstead, Gloria.'

'Remember remember,' Tyrone says.

But it's now, not then. She don't want to remember.

'Christmas soon,' says Suzanne.

'Soonish,' says Sam. 'Another month or so yet.'

'Better start saving your money,' says Tyrone.

'Christmas in December,' says Haider.

'Yeah,' Tyrone says.

Gloria leans forward and back. The woman beside her wriggles away slightly. Gloria looks out the windows in both directions, turning her head.

All these pubs are gonna close down soon, Jack says. It's all changing round here.

The pub that used to be opposite their bench is a betting shop now. She looks the other side of the road and sees the Tesco where the other pub used to be.

'All the pubs are closing down,' she says.

Sam looks at her.

Behind her, Tyrone laughs. 'Are you for real Gloria?' he says. 'Since when do you care if the pubs close down?'

She don't speak.

'When did you last go in a pub?' Tyrone says. He laughs again and shakes his head. 'You do come out with some funny stuff sometimes, I tell ya.'

Don't say I never do nothing for ya, says Jack. Gloria shakes her head. She claps her hands over her ears, on and off fast. It makes a dn dn dn dn dn dn dn dn noise and switches everything else off, all the other sounds. No one can talk to her or tell her nothing she don't want to hear. She can't hear nothing, just dn dn dn dn dn.

'Gloria,' Tyrone says.

Sam stands up and comes beside her. Puts a hand on her shoulder. The woman sitting beside the window gets up and pushes past Gloria and stands up by the door, holding onto the rail. Gloria can see the woman's hand gripping the rail in front of her, the knuckles all curled up and clean.

'Sorry,' Sam says to the woman, and the woman nods.

'Alright,' Sam says to Gloria. 'Calm, Gloria. Chill out.'

'Calm down Gloria,' Blessing calls across the aisle.

'Alright, Blessing,' Sam says.

Gloria taps her ears more. She rocks and makes the bus move backwards and forwards around her.

Sam nudges her over. 'Sit by the window,' she says. 'I'll sit next to you.'

Gloria pushes over to the window and leans her head on the cold glass. She keeps her hands on her ears but stops tapping on them.

'It's fine, Gloria,' Sam says. 'It's all fine.'

Tyrone leans forward. 'There's been too much behaviour already today,' he says. 'We don't need no more.'

'Especially not while we're out,' Sam says.

'Exactly,' Tyrone says.

The bus is moving. Gloria keeps watching the shops go past and the people walking up and down the pavements and all the lights. The bus goes on and on, slow. Jack's voice don't say nothing else. She thinks about the shops and the lights and being on the bus going forwards and forwards.

'I know we already spoke about this, but it's gonna be loud music and bangs and flashing lights tonight,' Sam says. 'Are you gonna be alright?'

'Bit late now,' Tyrone says.

'Yeah, that's helpful,' Sam says to him.

'You gonna be fine, ain't you Gloria?' Tyrone says from behind her.

Gloria don't say nothing. She keeps looking out the window.

'She's gonna be fine,' Tyrone says.

The doors open and shut and people get on and off. Gloria feels the cold around her ankles whenever they do. She keeps watching out the window. The bus turns up Green Street. The lights are better here, brighter and more colourful, shop windows full of glittering saris and frilly gold jewellery and people hunched over tables in busy restaurants. She presses her head on the window and watches everything outside, the lights of the shops and the people going by in the darkness.

Then she sees him.

Up the top end of the street, where the shops are thinning out and it's mostly houses, dark windows with thick curtains hoarding the light inside. The bus stops at the bus stop. The doors hiss open. People get off. Up the front, people get on. Gloria is looking out the window. It's just a flash she sees. A flash of recognition. The way he walks. The angry shoulders. Fast. The back of his head bent forward, the hair cut short.

She recognises. She knows that body. That walk.

He must of got out. Your fella. Ain't he come to say hello?

He's outside, just like the woman said. Walking along the pavement.

Gloria gets up. She pushes past Sam. She moves quick. Rushes to the door and steps out, down onto the pavement.

She stumbles but she don't fall. 'Gloria!' she hears Sam shout behind her, then, 'Shit!'

The doors close. The bus pulls away. She sees Tyrone, looking at her through the window and banging his hand on the glass, shouting something. But the bus moves away fast. And she don't hear what it is.

5

Gloria sees Jack's back picked out under street lights, his jacket reflecting the orange glow. His head is bent down, his arms held in front of him. She knows he is rolling a cigarette.

It has been a long long time since she last saw him. There have been a lot of Christmases. There have been plenty of summers, long hot days of doing nothing. The world has changed. Buildings have been built, and buildings have been knocked down, and shops have changed, and pubs have closed, and fences have gone or been built, and skylines look different. He always says the calendar was counting down to something, but it wasn't. It just keeps going and going and going.

His hair is thinner. The glow of skin shines in his scalp. She stays behind. She lets him keep walking a long way ahead. She don't know what he will look like now. She don't know if he will be happy to see her. She sees a tiny flare of light up ahead as he lights his cigarette, a little red fire dangling from his hand as he walks.

You ain't gonna leave me Gloria, he says in her head. The voice from a long time ago.

Ahead of her, he turns a corner. She walks fast and follows.

When she reaches him, she is going to stand behind him and say Jack, and he will turn around and see her, and he will smile. He will say I missed you. He will say I can relax now you're here. They will go for a walk together to see the fireworks and they will go and get chips.

When she reaches him, he will turn around and say Alright Gloria and all the years and the time that happened won't matter no more because he will still be the same. And so will she.

When she reaches him he will say Don't leave me Gloria. And he will say Do you want a Coke?

He will say I've never put my hands on you. Never once put my hands on you.

She stops walking. Just for a moment. She looks at him up ahead of her, his shoulders rolling side to side. She speeds up again and goes after him. Her feet tapping on the pavement, offbeat.

The street is cold and empty. Her walking, and him walking up ahead. Another man walks by on the other side of the road, going the opposite way to her and Jack. A car goes past.

Headlights. Yellow in the dark.

No. She don't want to remember that.

He will say Come with me if you like. I'll look after you.

She walks like catching up with him is what she wants to do.

Gloria remembers the last time she saw him, before just now. Jack getting pushed into a van. His arms twisted up behind his back.

Never once touched you have I? You answer me that.

Up ahead, Jack turns another corner.

Gloria walks faster. She don't want to walk slow and let him get away. If she lets him get away she might not ever see him again. Because he can go anywhere. She stays here but he can go wherever he likes. He might not ever come back to here again. He might go and run away with cans of food and make his den.

She thinks of his countdown to the year 2000, and how things reach too much. All the things inside her head. All the pictures happening again and again. The things he does. His shouting. The things she don't want to think about because they make her feel bad but she keeps thinking about them anyway. Because all the things remind her. Everything reminds her. Headlights at night or benches in the park or shouting or knuckles folded up and clenched with something gripped inside them. She can't stop things reminding her.

She don't know what he might do until he done it. And then he does it. And Mum says Gloria you ain't got no sense have you! You think you can trust some random bloke? You think nobody's gonna do nothing bad to you? And then

Gloria thinks that anyone can do anything, all the time. So she keeps quiet. When girls laugh in the park, when the man takes her handbag, when people say Give me money. When the lady on the TV asks her questions.

And she never says nothing about him no more. She never says nothing to Mum. Police ask her questions and it takes a long time. And she answers them quietly and with not many words. And then no more talking about Jack. In all this time she thinks and thinks about the good bits and the bad bits and all what happened. But she don't say nothing.

Gloria remembers Jack bossing her around saying Come here and saying Quiet and saying You ain't going nowhere, you ain't leaving me.

She is walking faster. He is in front of her. She could say to him Hello Jack and he could turn around and say I thought you wasn't gonna come back. He could buy her chips and take her back to his place and sit her down and talk and talk and talk to her. And boss her around and tell her to get him Coke and beer from the fridge. He could say I thought you was mad at me. And then he could say You ain't gonna leave me. He could grab her and push her. He could follow her outside. He could—

They reach the end of the street. She is close behind him. He turns onto the main road. Big old houses set back from the pavements. The cars rush past here. The cars go fast fast up this road. Lights spinning on puddles.

Jack is right in front of her now. Jack's back is right in front of her. The wide-open space between his shoulder blades. His body moving under the fabric of his coat. The shoulders swinging. The anger held in them, the rhythm. Ready to punch. The hurt he can do.

Gloria runs forward, arms out in front of her, hands spread wide. She pushes. She pushes hard. Hands thrum into his back. His spine bones jutting against her palms. The impact jars. Her wrists hurt.

He falls forward. He tries to move his legs to catch up. He trips and sprawls forward onto a car bonnet. Car screeches. Horn blares. The car skids to a stop. Jack rolls off. He lands in the road.

Cars stop, traffic stops moving.

The driver puts his head out the window. 'What the fuck are you doing?' he yells at the man.

The man groans.

Gloria stands watching. Her feet are stiff and solid on the pavement. She can't move.

The man groans. He lifts his hands up to his head.

He isn't Jack.

6

Gloria stands still. She looks at the man on the road. His face is different. He's not Jack. He moans again. The driver gets out of his car and says, 'You okay mate?'

The driver stands beside the man on the road, leaning over, bending forwards.

'I never saw you,' the driver says. 'You just ran out. You come from nowhere.' He turns to look at Gloria, standing still on the pavement. 'Did you see it?' he says. 'You must of seen it weren't my fault.'

Gloria don't speak.

The man on the road says something. The driver bends forward to hear.

A woman leans out of her car and says, 'Have you called an ambulance? Does he need an ambulance?'

'It weren't my fault,' the driver says.

'I'm saying have you called an ambulance?' the woman says.

Gloria's feet come alive. She starts to move. She takes two steps back.

The woman gets out of her car and slams the door shut. 'I'm calling an ambulance,' she says.

In her pocket, Gloria's phone starts to buzz. She feels it against the outside of her thigh. She don't take it out of her pocket.

Gloria's head is full and thick with now and then. The man lying in the road in front of her. Mr Miah. Jack. The things happening again the same way they did before, a car stopped in the road. Jack on the ground. Jack getting hurt.

A man leans out the car behind. 'She pushed him,' he says, pointing at Gloria. 'I seen the whole thing. She pushed him.'

The driver turns and looks at him, then back at Gloria.

'It weren't your fault mate,' the man in the car says. 'I seen what happened. She pushed him into the road.'

They both look at Gloria. The woman who is calling the ambulance kneels down next to the man on the floor.

'You pushed him?' the driver says.

Gloria watches the man on the floor. He rolls and shifts his body slightly, as though he is trying to wriggle in and get comfortable on the concrete. She hears him groan. She turns around. She turns around and starts walking.

'Hey!' the driver says. 'Hey!'

She starts to run.

Gloria don't like running. Running is hard. You have to

make sure your feet don't slip and stumble and it's faster than walking and your legs move more so there's more chance for things to go wrong. And you breathe hard, like your breath takes over all of you, and the whole top half of your body is just air pulling in and pushing out, and the whole bottom half of your body is legs flailing around trying to move fast and not trip, and it's difficult. Difficult to keep going.

The man is green and she runs across the road and up past the Iceland and up a hill, past the station and all the shops. There are lots of people walking up this road and she can't run no more because people are in the way and her legs are too tired and her breathing is too tired. In the distance there are bangs of fireworks going off but she don't look up to try and see the lights twinkle over the buildings and disappear. She keeps her eyes looking at the ground so she don't trip. When people are in front of her she says Excuse me, excuse me loudly so they know to get out the way. And she walks past them and around them, as fast as she can, to get away from the man on the ground who ain't Jack and the man in the car who says You pushed him? Hey!

You'll need to stick with me Gloria, Jack says in her head. When the shit hits the fan.

But Gloria is on her own. And she's pushed a man and made him fall and get hurt. The man lies on the ground and he don't get up. An ambulance is coming for him. Gloria has done something really bad and people saw and now she is running away.

Her head is all mixed up with what she just done and what Jack done and Mr Miah and the man on the ground and Jack getting hit. All these things and pictures mixing up, and she needs to keep moving and get away but they're staying with her inside her head.

She don't know what will happen to her because of what she just done, but she thinks she is in big trouble, the biggest trouble she's ever been in. She thinks she might go to prison even, the same as Jack. Prison is a bad place and they keep you locked up and they won't let you out and they put people there who do bad things. And because she hurt the man people will call the police and the police will chase her and catch her and arrest her and then they will send her to prison. Like Jack.

Gloria pushes past the people. She walks past the group of boys outside the chicken shop. Across the road there is a pub with people standing outside. She goes past the crossing and keeps walking under the railway bridge. There are two families walking in front of her, walking together. They are all talking to each other and they all know each other. They take up the whole width of the pavement, children and adults. They walk slow.

There's the weeeoooh of sirens in the distance.

'Excuse me,' she says, and the family don't move. She shouts it louder. 'Excuse me!'

A woman turns and looks at her and moves out the way. Gloria pushes through the little gap she opens up. The pavement ahead is clear and she runs again.

She is running away. She can't go back because the police will find her and more and more bad things will happen to her because she has done something really bad.

Have you ever slept outdoors? Jack says.

Gloria don't know where to go. She remembers all the times with Jack sitting in his room while he talks and talks about the Millennium and how when those three zeroes come on the calendar he will run away and he will know what to do. All the plans he makes and tells her about. Do you know how to build a fire? You've had it too soft. It won't be easy.

She remembers him showing her his knife. Taking it out and leaning over the side of the chair where she's sitting. Stroking the blade. Lots of things you can do with this, he says. It has rope around the handle and a piece of flint wrapped into it. Start a fire, he says. Use it for chopping things down. Use it for killing animals if you get hungry. He twists it so the blade catches the light in a bright sharp line. Good innit, Gloria?

Gloria don't have a knife. She thinks of all the things he says about taking when he runs away. A padlock, a decent rucksack, my knife, a gun. Food. Cans and that. She don't have a bag with her or nothing because she never knew this is going to happen today. She didn't know today is the day she will reach too much. She don't have nothing counting down like Jack does. He counts and counts, six months, five months.

All Gloria has is her keys and her blue furry purse with

money inside it. She wraps her hand around her purse, inside her pocket. She holds it and strokes it, feeling the coins shift inside its blue furry skin.

There's a shop. Gloria goes inside. Sweet wrappers and crisp packets shine from the shelves in red and blue and gold. The people going by outside are blurry black figures. Gloria looks on all the shelves. There's no knives. She picks up a big bottle of Coke and a packet of biscuits. The Coke is one pound and five p, so she will give two pounds for that. The packet of biscuits is eighty-nine p, so she will give one pound for that. Then she should get some money back from the man. She takes the Coke and the biscuits to the counter. She opens her blue fluffy purse and takes out three pound coins and hands them to the man in the shop.

'No, just this,' he says. He gives her one of the pound coins back. He opens the till and gives her three two p coins.

On the counter next to his till there's a lot of cigarette lighters, all standing up. They are all different colours, bright shiny plastic, green and fluorescent yellow and pink. Gloria looks at them. She remembers Jack scraping and clicking and leaning into the flame.

Gloria picks up a lighter. Clear blue plastic. She holds it up and tips it. Liquid moves inside.

The man reaches out and takes it from her. She thinks he's taking it away. He clicks at the side of it with his thumb and a big orange flame shoots out and then dies away. 'Working, see?' he says. 'You want it? Fifty.'

Gloria looks at him, thinking. She opens her hand and

looks at the gold-and-silver pound coin and the three brown two p coins.

'What's the matter Miss, you don't know money?' the man says. He laughs. He points at the pound coin. 'That,' he says. 'Just that.'

Gloria gives it to him. He opens the till and gives her a fifty p coin, big and silver with rounded edges. He gives her the lighter. She puts the coins and the lighter into her blue purse and pushes the purse back into her pocket. Her hands feel dry from the money, like it's left an extra skin on her skin.

'Like a bag?' the man says.

Gloria nods. That's another thing she needs.

He packs the biscuits and the Coke into a blue carrier bag and hands it to her. She takes it, feeling the weight pull through her arm and unbalance her slightly. It's not a rucksack but it's still a bag. She walks out of the shop, chimes tinkling on the door as she leaves.

She keeps walking, her hand around her purse, feeling the new shape of the lighter inside it. Jack never says about buying food in his plan. Jack says he will go on raids and take food. Or he might kill animals if he gets really desperate. But in Jack's plan everything has changed for everyone, and everything will be broken and you can go in places and raid. But now it's not the Millennium. Everything has changed for Gloria but it ain't changed for no one else.

Gloria thinks about the man she pushed. Things have changed for him too. She thought he was Jack but he weren't.

And she pushes him. And he ain't Jack. Is the man hurt? Is the man dead? He was moving and making noise. So he can't be dead. But Mr Miah was moving and making noise.

The thought chokes her. Mr Miah on the pavement moving and making noise. The image clear. His eyes and he looks at her and his noise.

Gloria keeps walking. She's shaking like she's cold, but it ain't cold. She concentrates on where her feet are going, on walking fast past all the people and not tripping over.

She reaches where there's no more shops or houses, just grass and open space on either side of the road. Wanstead Flats. Like a park but bigger. Like fields. All the people are walking up the road and turning onto the grass and walking across it. In the distance there's a glow of lights and the rhythmic bass of music. A fairground. Gloria walks onto the grass too, like everyone else. Her shoes slip in the mud. She stands still, waiting. People walk past her on either side.

There is water near here. There is a pond near here which could be like Jack's river. Gloria starts walking across the grass again. It's so dark away from the street lights she can't see where she's treading. There might be dog poo or anything. She has to go slowly. She walks up away from where most of the people are going.

Her foot twists hard into a hole. She falls over and lands hard on her front, the bag of Coke and biscuits slamming to the ground next to her. She can't breathe. Her lungs won't work. Her belly flails against the ground as she tries and tries to pull the air in. The world looms over her, the sky thick with orange clouds, the dark wet grass, the people walking away. She presses her hands into the mud. The mud sinks cold and wet around her fingers. There's a tight trapped feeling round her chest. She takes small breaths.

She lies there, trying not to cry. Her ankle is hurting. She presses her hands harder into the mud and lifts herself. She gets to her knees, then bends and gets to her feet. She picks up the carrier bag.

She starts walking again. Her ankle feels hot and soggy, soft like a balloon or a piece of sponge. Not good for leaning on. Her phone buzzes in her pocket again but she don't answer. She needs to concentrate on walking and on what she is going to do.

She walks away from the people, towards a group of trees. They are dark round outlines, grouped together like a shelter. She is going to go in there, in between the trees. She's been in there before, a long time ago, when it was warm and daytime. There's space in there. You can hide. And it's near a pond, near some water.

There's shouts and voices talking as people stream past and away towards the lights and music. She reaches the trees. There are bushes around them, brambles and stinging nettles. She pushes her way through, her ankles getting whipped and thorns poking through her trousers. She tugs her leg free of the thorns. Threads in her trousers break and tear, leaving a hole. The cold air rushes in against her leg. She stumbles and pushes her way through. Her legs are still walking in spite of the prickles and her sore ankle. She still don't cry.

The branches close over her head. It is very dark. She can hear the voices of people walking and the hum of music in the distance, and sirens, but it's all muffled. It's quieter. The loudest sound is the leaves rustling. And the cracks as twigs fall from trees. And the small things scurrying in bushes. Rats. Foxes.

Gloria can't see far. She walks in further under the trees. It's dark and no one will be able to see her. She likes trees because they are big and safe and strong, and because they change with the seasons so she knows when she is. She tries to remember this, how much she likes trees. The fear is in her neck, drowning her a bit. Making her heart go so fast she can feel it beating. Making breathing hard.

She sits down on the ground. Small twigs crack underneath her. Damp and cold seep up into her trousers. She is going to stay here. This is where she has found, somewhere quiet and alone, near some water. Outside of the city. She puts the carrier bag down beside her. Her supplies.

It's not easy getting sleep in the cold on hard ground, Jack says.

7

The sky explodes above her. Pretty floral bursts. Flashes between the trees.

Fireworks.

There is music happening. Gloria can hear the beat but not the words. She hears the crowd say Oooh in the distance as the lights burst into coloured pieces and fall downwards. The branches get in the way, break up the patterns and sparks, but she can see enough. Haider will be out there, and Sonam and Suzanne and Blessing, and Sam and Tyrone. Watching the fireworks and saying Ooh and Wow, standing together and feeling safe and excited watching the sky rip apart with light.

Gloria thinks of Jack looking at the sunset, saying Beautiful, this. She twists the cap open on the bottle of Coke and takes a drink. Sweet and sharp in the back of her throat. Her fingers cold and sticky where it fizzes over. She remembers Jack planning his room by the river. I'll have the bed in the corner, against the wall, so I can see everything from it soon as I wake up. A little fire over there if there's a chimney. Get the room warm when it's cold. Burn up all me old rubbish and that, keep it clean. I'll dig a hole outside for the toilet, cos the plumbing will probably all be fucked.

She needs to pee. She can't ignore it any longer. There are no toilets. The cold ain't helping.

She gets up and walks a little bit away from where she was sitting, hobbling on her sore ankle and wincing to herself. She's got nothing to dig a hole with and anyway she can't wait. She pulls down her trousers and her pants and squats. It feels strange, peeing outdoors in the dark. She has nothing to wipe with and she can't wash her hands. Even though you should always wash your hands. But she can't.

She goes back to where she was sitting. Gold and silver fireworks explode, rocking her ears. But the loud noise don't scare her. It don't irritate and squirm inside her brain. It's clean and bold. She sits hidden in the dark, sipping her Coke. She opens the packet of biscuits and eats one.

You have to find a bed, Jack says. You have to make it out of anything. Dried bits of wood. Crates or old plastic bottles or whatever. You want some air between you and the ground, that's the point. Keep you warm, sort of thing. Like insulation. But she don't know where to start. The ground is cold and hard and it's seeping into her, making her muscles ache and making her not want to move.

Gloria thinks about Jack's plan. She thinks about fire.

She opens her purse and gets out the lighter. She scrapes her fingers on the side of it like she's seen him do. It makes a scraping clicking noise but nothing happens. She remembers Jack when his lighter won't work and how he keeps clicking it and clicking it, scrape scrape scrape and then the hiss and the flame. She tries again. She presses harder, the small metal wheel digging into her thumb. A burst of orange sparks fly out. They disappear straight away. She does it again. A flame appears. She watches it. It is orange at the top and blue at the bottom. It huddles down in the cold. It waves at her then goes.

Just dry bits of wood and that.

The fireworks break open the sky above her. She puts the lighter in her lap and reaches out to the ground at her sides. She closes her hands on twigs and leaves. The leaves fold and break in her hands, wet and cold. They stick to her skin and make her hands colder. She pushes them up into a small pile, sweeping her hands from the side to the front like she is playing with sand. She presses and pats it, creating a mound.

She tries again. She holds the lighter down to the pile of leaves and clicks it. A flame bursts out. Not as big as the one the man got in the shop. It stays low to the lighter. She holds the lighter so a leaf is touching it, so the leaf is right inside the flame. The orange of the flame lights up the pile of brown leaves and twigs and part of the ground, showing big pieces of dark shadow hidden inside the pile. Gloria holds the lighter where it is, pressing on it so the flame don't go out.

Her thumb burns. She lets go and drops the lighter.

A burst from the fireworks lights up the ground. She sees the lighter. She picks it up and holds it. The metal bit is very very hot. She holds the plastic bit.

She realises the leaves and twigs will not catch fire. Because they ain't dry. She don't have dry bits of wood. Everything is wet because it was raining before. She's stuck with the cold. She takes her purse out of her pocket and puts the lighter back.

She pulls her knees into her chest. Her ankle is hurting. She is shivering from the cold Coke and the cold ground. It's not easy. Jack's voice is in her head all the time, talking to her. Maybe she won't ever see him again. Maybe she has really hurt the man. Maybe she will get caught and go to prison. Maybe in prison she will meet Jack. But Jack is outside again, that's what the woman said.

She can't hear the music properly. She don't know what the words are. All the songs sound the same from here, simple meaningless beats shaking the air. A twig snaps behind her and it makes her jump. She turns around but she can't see nothing. Only the dark outline of trees. She shivers. Her legs and her teeth vibrating. The Coke is sharp and sweet on the back of her throat. The taste reminds her of summer. Jack standing by the window. His face bright in front of her.

Fireworks overhead change. They turn into round white ones that scribble circles on the sky with a noise like crayon on paper.

Mr Miah says Are you okay? Mr Miah says Do you want a lift love? Mr Miah wants her to get in the car and he would drive her away and drive her home. But Gloria don't move.

But Jack is holding her arm. Holding too tight. You're hurting her.

Mr Miah's face goes hard like stone. Mr Miah's face goes pale pale pale. Mr Miah's head hits the ground.

No.

She rocks. She can change the motion of the night around her.

The ground is making her so cold. All her muscles shiver.

Jack says You have to find a bed. You have to make it out of anything.

Gloria pushed a man. Her hands shove into his back hard. The man ain't Jack. The man is just a man. The man could be anyone. Maybe he's a man like Mr Miah who wants to help. She remembers the man's face on the ground, screwed up, his eyes closed, his body rolling over. She remembers the feeling in her hands, tingling in her palms that never satisfy until they slam against his back. She has to do it. Her hands make her do it, they want to do it and she follows. They pull her along. Take the bad flash inside of her and push it into him. But it don't go from her. It's still there with her and now it's on him too. She just made it more. Two instead of one.

Maybe the man is okay. Maybe he got up and walked away.

Maybe he is in hospital.

Maybe he ain't dead.

She will be in big trouble. She will get arrested and she will go to prison.

It was a bad thing to do. It was a bad thing she done.

If the police catch her they'll hit her. Like they hit Jack. She thinks of when the police come and get Jack. The police hitting and hitting with their sticks and Jack cries out. Blue lights and sirens. Blue flashes, staining the blue of the night. Sirens screaming rhythm. Jack looks at Gloria but he don't move. He looks at her when the sirens are coming and when the blue light is on them both, flashing them on and off, whipping through dark and light and dark and light. Flashing on Mr Miah lying on the floor, the pale of his face. Shining on his half-open eyes, the dark wet pool of his blood. Splintering on the bits of broken glass on the pavement. Gloria has breath and tears coming in and out of her. She is bent over with the effort to breathe. The blue light is shining in Jack's eyes. The little flecks of blood on his face look black.

And Mr Miah is there on the floor.

Gloria don't forget it ever.

The van pulls up across the road, sirens screaming and screaming, blue light flashing. The door slides open, kssssh, and the uniform men rush out, slam of boots on the tarmac.

Jack turns and starts to run then. His naked back reflecting blue light. He runs fast, his bare feet pounding the road. The men run after him.

'Police,' the men shout. 'Stop.'

The uniform men run fast after Jack. They hurl themselves after him. One man leaps and grabs him.

More men come. Jack twists and wriggles and ducks. Gloria sees him, his body, his head sliding out from under their arms and twisting away then down. Down. He has blood on him. Blood staining his jeans.

They land on him and he crashes into the road. His skin crashes and grinds into the tarmac on the road and they are on top of him.

The men are at Mr Miah. They kneel down beside Mr Miah. They are looking at him and looking at the blood and pulling rubber gloves onto their hands and feeling his neck. Pressing and pounding on his chest up and down, squeezing him all the way in and out like if you step on the chest of a doll. Mr Miah's head rolls side to side with how hard they pressing on him.

The men are at Gloria. They are beside her. One of them is. And she screams and cries to cover up everything and to hide it from herself. To hide it with noise and tears. The man puts his hands on her and holds his hand on her shoulder and pulls her back and round. She pulls away from his hand and turns back to look at Jack and Mr Miah. She wants to make noise and scream. She don't want no one to stop her.

The men are on Jack. They are on Jack, on top of him, he is lying on the ground, the man is on top of him and other men are standing by him. The men have black sticks and they hit him. They swing the sticks up and down and hit into Jack, squashing him into the tarmac, and he cries. He is crying with tears on his face and he screams and shouts out when the sticks hit into him.

She watches him cry. She stops shouting so she can listen to him scream when the sticks hit into him. The police holds Jack's arm and twists it up behind his back and holds it there, pushes it harder, and Jack rolls on the ground trying to move so he can change how his arm is and stop it pulling and breaking. But the police kneels on him so he can't move. Jack's face twists up and he shouts his sobs loud into the air. Gloria remembers his hands on her neck. She remembers him pressing her on the bed. Shut up Gloria shut up! You ain't going nowhere. You ain't leaving me.

She watches Jack on the ground cry. She watches Jack on the ground get hit. She watches Jack on the ground get his arm all twisted and hurt. The man takes out handcuffs and holds both of Jack's arms and pushes them high together and handcuffs both of Jack's wrists. Then he stands up. He kicks Jack. Gloria watches.

They are pressing on Mr Miah still. They put a cover over Mr Miah's mouth and blow into it and they press on his chest. The hard pressing on his chest is making him bounce and move and making thick sludgy ripples slide through the blood pooled around him. Little dribbles of blood push up through his T-shirt whenever they press on his chest.

Gloria stops looking at Mr Miah. She looks over at Jack. She watches Jack's face twisting and crying. Someone is still holding her arm. He puts his hand on her shoulder. He says, 'What's your name?'

8

The light fades. The noise finishes and the music stops. There are no more fireworks.

Gloria is so cold. The night didn't seem cold before, but when you stay still in it, it gets to you. It makes you get cold and you don't even know until you're freezing. Everything feels damp. She bites her arm. She bites hard, sacrificing her arm to make her mouth feel better. There is soft and warmth around her teeth and sharp and pain in her arm. All of the feelings mash together inside her body.

Her phone vibrates in her pocket. Her leg is almost numb, the vibration feels odd, like it's happening far away. She gets her phone out and looks at the bright screen. Mum, it says. Gloria can read it. She looks at the phone buzzing and buzzing in her hand. If she presses the green-phone button her mum will be talking to her. She waits and looks at it. She don't know what she will say and she don't want to hear no words. After a bit the phone stops vibrating. The screen goes dark again.

Voices begin to grow from beyond the trees. People coming closer. Laughing and talking. She gets up. Her legs are numb and soft. She stands among the trees, waiting. She likes the sound of all the voices, turning into one solid blur with words emerging and retreating. She listens. She rocks again, gently.

Mum Mum did you see how high I went? Cor I went all the way up—

Nah allow it fam I ain't on that you know—

Yeah I told him I said—

Manor Park? Is it. I—

Ah she never! No, she never!

Laughter and shouts. Pops and flurries of different languages. Shapes of people moving on the other side of the trees. The lights of different phone torches picking their way across the grass.

Rain starts. Fat bold drops plummeting through the trees. It happens fast, coming down hard from nowhere. Landing cold on her hands and cheeks. She pulls her hood up. Water touches the back of her neck. Water comes through the leaves. The ground softening to mud. She shivers, her body wriggling and shuddering. She wants to be warm.

She has no shelter. All her clothes will get all wet. And she won't get dry again because it's cold outside. She can't stay here. She has to go somewhere else where she can be warm and dry. You've had it too soft. She shakes her head to rid herself of Jack's voice. She needs to hide indoors. Maybe she can hide at Mum's. Because it's not where she lives. So if police want to arrest her she can go to her mum's instead and they won't find her. But her mum might be cross too because of what she did to the man.

Gloria starts to walk towards the trees, to where she pushed through the bushes to get in. Her feet stick and slip in the mud. Her ankle is hurting her. Her shoe lets in water. The shock of it is extra cold against her cold foot. Her sock getting soggy, her foot flooded in water. A few more steps and the water in her shoe warms up a little, like her shoe is a bath. Then she treads in another puddle and a new rush of cold seeps in. You can't walk around like that Gloria, you look a mess. She knows she needs new shoes. Her mum is always saying.

She pushes through the trees and into the low bushes. A stinging nettle stings her hand. The sting feels worse in the wet, raw and spiteful. Brambles catch her and pull her back, picking more threads from her trousers. There's people walking across the grass. Loads and loads and loads of them. In groups. Everyone talking. People with umbrellas, huddling together underneath them, holding their phone torches out to illuminate the ground.

Over towards the road a group of boys break out into shouts and jerky movements. They push each other, moving towards and away from each other like magnets. Gloria can hear odd words–

Nah bruv!

Nah bruv!

Yo what the fuck!

Heads angle in their direction, curious, a bit afraid. Gloria's heart goes faster. She watches. People do things. People stab and people throw acid and shoot. People hurt. She don't want no trouble. She's had enough trouble.

The boys' voices sound frightened and excited all at once. As though they think something might happen, something more than walking to somewhere and walking back again. Something that could change things. Gloria looks over. She waits. She don't want to move more until she knows what she's walking into.

One of the boys starts shouting really loud. Just yelling, a dull noise, over and over again. 'AAAAAAAAAAH! AAAAAAAAAAAH! AAAAAAAAAAH!'

Gloria jumps. There is more shouting. Young male voices stripped raw. 'Fuck man! Fuck! Yo Ray! Yo Ray! Ray! No fucking—'

'Oh FUCK!' one of the fighting boys screams, his voice shrieking above the crowd. People are huddling in, drawing in around the sound. Gloria cannot see past them to see what's going on. She can just hear the distress and violence in the air.

She's trembling.

Sirens. Flashing blue lights. A car drives onto the grass. It don't slow for the crowd. People scream and jump out of the way. People shout. 'Fucking pricks! You nearly fucking killed someone! Fucking pigs.'

More blue lights. The crowd move. A van comes, and another van. The bright orange strip down the side, gleaming. Men in uniform get out and walk into the crowd. Gloria cannot see what is happening. There's shouting and more noise and more noise. Everything is around her. Bad things and blue flashing lights and shouting. Gloria puts her hands on her ears. She turns and starts walking back inside the trees. She can't go out now. Otherwise the police will catch her.

Someone comes into the trees near her. Crashing and rushing. Breathing hard. Gasping breath. The outline of a boy. He holds onto a tree then rushes in further, into the wet bushes. He crouches down. His breath is rasping. She stays still. She stays very very still.

The boy turns and sees her. 'What the fuck you looking at man?' he shouts. He shouts it hard and fast and low. Blue lights flash on and off outside the trees. They catch his face. His face is covered. He's wearing a hood and a hat that comes all the way down and covers his whole face, a smooth outline. There is a hole in the hat for his eyes. His eyes shine in the blue light. 'Say a fucking word,' the boy says.

Outside is shouting and noise. The boy is low to the ground. The ground is wet. The boy must be getting wet from the rain, like Gloria is. He is shaking. His teeth are chattering together.

'I swear you open your mouth you're fucking dead,' the boy says. He sounds so angry and he sounds like he will cry as well. Gloria keeps her mouth closed. She knows bad things people can do.

The boy's phone starts to ring. 'Shit,' he says. He scrambles and silences it.

There are lights through the trees. Round white lights. Police walkie-talkies. Radios crackling and talking.

'Get down,' the boy says. He says it low and hissing. Gloria don't move. She is too afraid.

The boy crawls. He crawls and wriggles through the mud towards her. His tracksuit bottoms are light grey. They get caught on a plant and start to come down and he lays down and reaches back and hoists them up again. He comes to Gloria. He reaches up to her with his hand and pulls on her arm hard. He's pulling her like the way she sees children pulling their mums when they want something. He pulls so hard he pulls her down and she sits in the cold mud. It sinks through her trousers and pants. She starts shivering.

'Stay down,' the boy growls at her. 'They see you, they see me.'

She sits where she is. She puts her head down.

The boy lays back in the mud. He kisses his teeth. 'Mud on my jacket,' he says.

Gloria looks at him. She can't see his nose or his mouth, just eyes inside a hat that comes all the way down. The rain slows but keeps coming. There's voices and shouting and radios. Yeah roger that.

'I gotta get the fuck out of here,' the boy says. He's talking to her so quiet. 'I ain't going pen. Oh shit!' He starts crying. He starts rocking back and forth, the same way Gloria does sometimes. 'They can fucking do me just for being there,' he says. Crying eyes inside a hat.

He pushes the hat up and she sees his face. He looks like Jack, his face is the same, it moves the same way. It's hard and solid but it still moves fast and shows lots of feelings in a twitchy jerky way, like his body does too. And you can see that one day everything will break.

The boy wipes his face with his hand. 'What you looking at?' he says. 'What you fucking looking at fucking bitch?'

Gloria don't like that. Everything's a lot. He's made her get more cold and made her sit down in the mud and now he's calling her bitch. 'Shut up,' she says.

He laughs. It's a soft quiet laugh like a whisper. 'Oh you speak,' he says.

Everybody says that. Everybody says that to Gloria. Everybody says Why don't you speak or Do you speak or You should speak more or Can't you speak? Even this boy with his hat on his face. Even Jack says You don't talk much. She's mad. She's so mad and tired of everyone talking about words and speaking and whether she does it enough and how she should be different. She screams. She screams at the boy, one shout, one blast, just AAAH! No words.

The boy jumps up. He jumps up from the ground and lands on her, his hand on her mouth, pressing hard hard on her mouth and nose, ramming her lips into her teeth. Her head's pressed on the ground. Rain drips on her forehead.

There is a stick poking into her head. And the boy's lying on top of her, his body hard on hers. He wriggles around with one hand and the other hand is still pressed hard on her mouth. It really hurts and there is blood in her mouth, more and more of it coming from her lips. And with the hand that isn't on her mouth he brings up a knife and he puts it in front of her eyes. He says, 'I will hurt you. I will cut you. Keep your mouth shut.'

She keeps her eyes open. She looks at the knife. There are tiny lights moving on it, reflections from the blue lights flashing. There is blood on it. She wants him off her. She wants him to get his hands off her and get the knife away from her. She pushes and pushes at him. He presses his hand hard into her mouth.

He's like Jack.

Scream and I'll hurt you. You think I don't mean it? I really fucking mean it.

He's like Jack. He's pressing her and holding her and he has a knife.

'Stop moving man what's wrong with you,' he says. 'I just nearly killed somebody. Maybe I did kill somebody.' He's whispering. 'It's all fucked,' he says.

His eyes widen. He laughs and laughs, quiet laughter that sounds like rain landing on a puddle.

'It's so fucked,' the boy says.

She remembers Jack pushing her on the bed, the sheets smelling of old sweat. Jack squeezing his hands on her neck saying Stay still don't cry. She wants the hands off her. The feeling is hot and strong inside her belly and chest, it's bursting out of her, she don't want Jack and she don't want this boy on her. She bucks and strains. She pulls her lips back and the flesh of his hand comes between her teeth and she bites hard. His skin is soft and smooth and cold and wet. She tastes mud. She tastes someone else's blood in her mouth. His skin bursts between her teeth. She knows it hurts him, she can guess how it feels because of all the times she bites her own hand and dares herself harder and harder and don't quite break the skin or breaks it a bit, she can feel his pain in her own hand, and her mouth feels strange, sore and salty and metal. He calls out, a sharp grunt AHH! Her teeth feel warm and sated. The boy pulls his hand away and her teeth click together. He is still sitting on her. The knife is over her head. She screams. She screams and screams and screams. She turns sideways so she can't see the knife. Her face is in leaves and mud. She don't care. She'd rather see leaves and mud than his knife and his face. The boy grabs her and shakes her and says Shut up shut up and she keeps screaming. The cold wet of the ground against her face. She's not shutting up for no one who's pressing her down and pushing her and hurting her. She don't care. Everything has to go and leave her, no body no person touching her and talking to her. Just cold wet ground. Just mud. She can go deep in it. Insects and worms on her. She'll go there when she dies and she wants it now, she wants everything finished and no more people telling her to speak or to shut up. No more words talking. No more skin touching her. The boy can't stop her screaming. Only if he kills her. If he puts the knife in her like Jack did Mr Miah, one big sweeping motion, and she don't care. If he does that she don't care.

9

Gloria roars out another scream but her throat feels tired and the sound crumples and goes away. She tries again and it's dry like a loud whisper.

The boy goes. The weight of the boy and the sharp bones of his knees go from off her. She hears running and crashing, sticks crunching. There is more crashing and ripping and tearing, voices and walkie-talkies, static and voices flat through radios, not spoken out loud from mouths. She holds onto the mud, her hands cold and wet. Her fingers digging in the mud. There's blue lights and white dot lights. She looks at a leaf right in front of her eye. When the police come they will hurt her like they hurt Jack. She's frightened and she don't care. Both things at once. There's boots coming and men shout Police Police. The men are police shouting their own name. She should shout Gloria but she don't. She waits on the ground. She's not quiet because someone's told her to be quiet. She's quiet because she don't want to speak. A light shines on her. It makes dark shadows come inside the brown leaves. She shuts her eyes tight. Someone shouts Stand up! Gloria pushes her hands on her ears. Her eyes are closed and her ears are closed. She can still see light, she can see bright light there and then gone and then there again. Someone presses on her pockets and she screams. Someone presses her all over, all over her body and she screams again and takes her hands off her ears and pushes on the hands and the hands grab her wrists. They feel tacky and smooth and cold. She opens her eyes. A police lady is looking at her and says, 'Calm down. You need to calm down. If you assault me I will arrest you.' She says it loud and hard. She has a light on her chest from her mobile and the light shines up and makes her chin and under her nose bright so her face looks strange. The woman police says, 'What's happened? Has someone hurt you? Are you hurt anywhere?' She's talking hard and bossy. Gloria tries to pull her wrists away. The woman holds on. The woman's hands have blue plastic gloves on them. Tight and smooth. 'Calm down,' the woman says. 'Breathe with me, okay, in and out.' Gloria pulls her hands away from the blue plastic hands and the woman lets go. Gloria curls her hands up tight by her neck so no one can touch her and grab her wrists. She stays still on the ground. The woman police stays still too. The woman police has a bright yellow jacket on with water on it. The water shines blue and white in beads. There is two more police standing near her.

'Is this the misper?' a man police says.

'What's your name?' the woman police says. 'What's your name?'

'Gloria,' the man police says. 'Are you Gloria?'

Gloria won't move. She stays still with her hands up tight round her neck. Her legs are cold and can't move.

'Stand up,' the woman says.

The man comes closer. Gloria can see his face. A round hole for his mouth and round holes for his eyes. 'We can take you to your carer, Gloria,' he says. 'We can take you to Tyrone.' He waits. Then he says, 'Stand up and come with us.'

'We know you can understand us,' the woman says. 'Will you stand up or will we help you to stand up?'

Gloria don't move. The man police grabs her arm. She can feel the hardness of his hands through her coat as he lifts her and her weight goes against his hands. The woman police holds her other arm and pulls. Gloria squeezes her eyes closed. She is standing up and they are holding her arms. Her foot is wet in her busted trainer. Her legs are cold and won't work properly. Her trousers are damp on her shins. The police are holding on her arms too tight. The police start walking. They pull her and she walks too. Her ankle hurts. Her feet trip on plants. The police hold her. They stop her from falling over.

'Oops. We've got you,' the woman says.

'We're going to see Tyrone,' the man says.

She opens her eyes. Her heart is pounding so hard. Her throat is too tight and dry to make noise. There's sticks and twigs and trees and hands holding her arms. She shakes. She's cold. Her teeth chatter and chatter. She shakes even while she's walking. The police step and she has to step too because they are holding her too tight. The police push and steer her. They go through the trees out onto the grass.

People look over. The crowd begins to curl around Gloria and the police. People take out their phones and hold them up, pointing them at Gloria and the police. Little points of light in the dark.

The police keep walking and Gloria walks too, in between them. They're holding on her arms tight. 'Back up back up,' the man police shouts at the people.

The crowd move to let them walk through.

'Gloria,' the man police says in her ear. 'You need to stay calm.' He is talking low and quiet, close to her. He is walking beside and behind her. He is all around her like a wall. If she tries to go away she knows he'll be there, stopping her. He's bigger than her. He's solid. He's wider than Jack. 'It's okay, Gloria,' he says.

The people don't follow them. They point the lights at Gloria while she walks away with the police. Gloria keeps quiet. But she's not calm. Her whole body is tense. Her muscles are trembling. She's waiting waiting waiting to see what comes next.

At the edge of the grass police cars and police vans are parked up. The police walk her over to one of the cars. The blue and green patches on its side gleam, throwing bits of light back at her.

Tyrone gets out the police car. And another police gets out the car, a woman. Tyrone and the police both stand by the car and look at Gloria.

'Gloria,' Tyrone says. He is frowning.

She looks at him. Her chest calms down a bit seeing him. The police relax their hands on her arms. One of the police pats her shoulder.

Gloria don't know why Tyrone was in the car. He is with Sam and Haider and Sonam and Blessing and Suzanne. They are watching the fireworks and then they are going home. He ain't with the police. He don't go in police cars.

'What were you thinking Gloria?' Tyrone says. 'Why did you run away? We've all been worried about you. I've had to tell Sharifah. We've had to call the police.' He sighs and looks at her. 'Are you alright?' he says. 'Where have you been?'

Gloria don't speak.

'We'll have to have a proper talk about this when we get back,' Tyrone says. 'Sharifah ain't happy you know. How can we manage trips if you're gonna do a runner?'

Gloria pulls her arms away from the police and they don't hold on. But they still stand very close.

'I've had to leave Sam with the others,' Tyrone says. 'She's by herself managing with everyone. She shouldn't have to do that. What were you thinking?'

Gloria don't speak. Suddenly she remembers she's left her Coke and biscuits in the trees. She spent nearly two pounds on them.

'Come on,' Tyrone says, sighing. 'We're gonna have to get the bus back.'

The woman police beside Tyrone moves, steps forward. 'Sorry sir,' she says. 'We can't let her go just yet.'

'What do you mean?' Tyrone says.

'We need to talk to Gloria in connection with an earlier incident,' the woman says.

Gloria's stomach clenches and drops. The calm that started to happen when she saw Tyrone goes away. Her heart beats hard. She watches Tyrone. She waits for him to change things.

Tyrone is frowning. 'What earlier incident?' he says. 'What's happened? She okay?'

'She's a suspect,' the woman says.

'A su— what?' Tyrone is staring at the woman, at the police beside Gloria, and then at Gloria. 'Jesus Christ, a suspect?' he says. 'Suspected of what?'

Gloria watches Tyrone. Gloria keeps looking at him. Because Tyrone knows her and Tyrone makes her cups of tea and helps her get food and put her laundry in the washing machine and plan how to get to places. Tyrone knows. He will know what to do. She waits for Tyrone to tell her It's okay Gloria and that she shouldn't worry.

'Someone matching her description was involved in an assault earlier,' the woman says.

'Someone matching her description?' Tyrone says, his voice getting louder. 'What, grey jogging bottoms and a black coat? Do me a favour.' He points a thumb at Gloria.

205

'You know she's got a learning disability,' he says. 'She ain't about to assault anyone. She ain't… This is a joke,' he says.

'We will need to speak to her down at the station,' the woman says. 'She will need to be interviewed under caution.'

'You understand that, Gloria?' the lady standing beside her says, looking at Gloria. 'We need to interview you. We need to ask you questions.'

The lady raises her eyebrows and smiles. Gloria feels the man beside her move. She feels him ready to move if she runs. Her ankle is hurting. She thinks the man police beside her will pull out a stick to hit her. She turns to look but he hasn't. He is just standing, waiting. His hands by his sides.

'I can't believe this,' Tyrone says.

Nobody says anything.

'Can I just call my manager?' Tyrone says. 'Can you just wait while I do that?'

The lady nods. 'Of course, sir,' she says, gesturing.

Tyrone gets his phone out of his pocket and dials. He puts the phone to his ear and turns away, towards the car. Gloria can still hear him talking but she can't hear what he's saying. Anna salt anna salt. She starts to rock to try and make things move the way she wants them to.

'Do you wanna get in the car, Gloria?' the man says from beside her. He puts a hand on her back so she can't rock no more because his hand presses against her and stops her. He nudges her forwards. She goes a little way, walking towards Tyrone. Then she stops. She don't want to go with them at all. They might take her to prison. She wants to go home.

The woman police comes closer to Gloria. She puts her hand on Gloria's arm again. 'Get in the car, Gloria,' the woman police says. 'We need to ask you some questions.'

'Am I going prison?' Gloria says.

Tyrone turns round from his phone call. '"Am I going prison?" No, you ain't going prison, Gloria,' he says. 'She's asking if she's going prison,' he says, down the phone. He shakes his head.

'You're not going to prison, Gloria,' the lady says. 'Just to the police station. We just need to take you to the police station and ask you some questions.'

'Okay. Yeah I will. Talk to you later. Bye,' Tyrone says down the phone. Then he ends the call and puts his phone back in his pocket. 'It's fine, Gloria,' he says. 'It's fine.'

Gloria looks at him. She's thinking different things, pictures of the man falling and the boy with the knife and Jack shouting out on the floor and Jack getting pushed in a cage in the van, his back all twisted because his arms are pushed up.

'Just give me your hands, Gloria,' the lady says.

Gloria don't move. Why ain't they arresting the boy? He pushed her and he put his knife in front of her face.

'Nah, you don't need to,' Tyrone says. 'You don't need to, she'll be fine.'

The lady don't look at him. She reaches out towards Gloria. She grabs her hand round Gloria's wrist. Holding tight but not too tight. Her hand is cold. She pulls Gloria's arm forward. She reaches to her belt where things are looped around her waist. She lifts up handcuffs from the belt. 'I'm not gonna hurt you. They don't hurt, Gloria,' she says. She presses one silver ring on Gloria's wrist and then Gloria's wrist is caught inside it. A cold metal circle. 'They just go on your wrists. Not too tight,' the police says. The circle touches Gloria at the sides and bottom of her wrist but not at the top. 'It's for everyone's sake okay? To keep everyone safe.' The police presses the other circle on Gloria's other wrist. She holds both of Gloria's hands together. She smiles at Gloria, her lips smearing across her face in a red curve.

Gloria feels everything fluttering and pounding, problems and trouble stuck inside her, wanting to burst out and move away. She tries to move her hands apart but she can't. The loops are hard around her wrists, keeping her hands stuck together. She flaps her fingers open and closed and pulls. She makes a noise, a growling shouting noise to show she's stuck and scared. The police is holding Gloria's arm. She stands close, close, her grip solid and tight. Gloria hears her swallow, the saliva clicking in her throat. Gloria shakes her head to try and block the sound cos she can't put her hands on her ears.

Tyrone comes closer. 'It's fine Gloria,' he says quietly. 'It's fine, just do what she says.'

Fine its fine its fine its.

The man police moves around from behind her, coming round so she can see him. He stands near Tyrone.

Gloria's hands are held together. A heavy hard bracelet on each hand. They can't move apart. They can't push closer together. They don't move where she tries to move, they are stuck together, fixed at her wrists, tight and solid. She makes the noise again. Panic and trap. She tries to lift her hands to her face and back down but the woman police holds her arm tight and presses to stop her moving. 'Okay calm down Gloria calm down Gloria,' the woman police says loudly.

Tears start in Gloria's eyes. The metal around her wrists shines, lines of orange and blue light moving on its surface from the street lights and the police cars.

Tyrone stands really close. His arm pressing on hers. He puts his hand on her back.

She breathes fast. She shakes her arms. The police lady holds on tighter. 'You need to stay calm,' she says.

'Okay,' Tyrone says to the police, putting one hand out. 'It's okay. She's okay. Gloria,' he says quietly. His voice is tense. 'Calm. Please be calm. Stay still. I know it's scary, but don't worry Gloria, okay? You're not gonna get hurt. It'll all get sorted out. You just need to stay still. Do as you're told. For the moment. Please, okay? Trust me. Just do what they say.'

Pleaseokay pleaseokay.

Tyrone is rubbing her back. She can feel the warmth and regular pressure, stroking up and down, broad and gentle, showing her where she is. 'Please okay,' she says, liking how the words sound, the rhythm of it. Tears spill on her cheeks.

'Please okay,' Tyrone says back to her. He smiles at her.

The police are watching. The lady police is still holding her arm, a bit less tight.

'Keep your arms still,' Tyrone says. 'No noise. Just be calm. It won't be long.'

'It's fine, Gloria. If you get in the car,' the lady says. 'We can take them off again at the station. We'll be as quick as we can.' She pulls on Gloria's arm gently.

Tyrone stops rubbing her back. 'Okay?' he says. 'Just be cool.'

Gloria keeps her arms still, holding them in front of her, newly heavy with the weight of the handcuffs. She stays still. The lady has her hand on Gloria's arm loose now. Gloria concentrates to makes the panic in her chest stay where it is and not come bursting out in noise or movement. She blinks and tears fall. Jack's handcuffs was at his back but hers are on the front. Maybe it means something different. Maybe she ain't in as much trouble.

'You coming with us sir?' the man says to Tyrone.

'Yeah,' Tyrone says. 'Yeah, I'm coming.'

'Okay,' the man says. 'Well, if we all get in the car.' He gestures like he is letting them into his home.

'Come on,' Tyrone says to Gloria really quietly. The lady police leads her slowly, holding her arm. They walk a few steps to the car. Gloria stares at the ground to see where the bumps and holes in the grass are. It's hard balancing with her hands stuck in front of her. Her breath is coming fast.

The lady opens the car door, onto the back seat.

Gloria looks at Tyrone to see if she should get in the car. She feels sick. She tastes the Coke in her throat.

Tyrone nods at her.

'If you get in first,' the woman says to Tyrone, 'and then if you get in after him, Gloria.'

Tyrone stoops and shifts, folds himself into the car and slides along the seat.

'And then you,' the lady says to Gloria.

Gloria don't move.

Tyrone leans forward. She looks at him. 'Come on Gloria,' he says. 'The sooner we do it, the sooner it's done.'

Gloria steps forward. She lifts her leg to get into the car and she wobbles because of her hands being caught together. The lady police holds her shoulder. Gloria leans against her. She steps her foot into the car. She leans forward and pushes herself into the seat, falling a bit. The lady's hand is touching Gloria's head. Gloria's cheek presses into Tyrone's shoulder. She sits up.

'Shuffle over Gloria,' the lady says.

Gloria wriggles over closer to Tyrone so his shoulder and arm is touching hers. The woman police gets in after her. She leans over Gloria and clips the seat belt across her. The man police closes the door. He gets in the front seat. He starts the engine. The gentle motion of it thrums through the seat. Gloria's wrists sit in her lap heavy, the silver around them shining.

'Gloria,' the woman police says. 'I need to say this to you, okay? I need to tell you that I am arresting you on suspicion of assault occasioning actual bodily harm. You do not have to say anything, but it may harm your defence if you do not mention when questioned something which you later rely on in court. Anything you do say may be given in evidence.'

Gloria has heard this on the telly a lot. The police say it when they catch people.

'Jesus Christ,' Tyrone says.

'It's the law for me to tell you that,' the lady says.

'Actual bodily harm?' Tyrone says. 'Are you guys for real?'

Bodily arm bodily arm.

'Let's wait until we get to the station shall we?' the lady says.

Tyrone shakes his head.

The car pulls out. They drive down the road. Gloria looks through the windscreen. There are little beads of rain on the glass, and the orange and red of passing headlights makes them shine like jewels. The windscreen wipers keep brushing them away and more keep coming. Gloria stares at them. Bodily arm bodily arm. She presses her tongue against the side of her teeth hard so she feels the smooth and rough and the scraping pain, but it's not enough. She can't hide in the sensation.

10

Somewhere small, where I can see all the exits and entrances, Jack says. So I can keep an eye.

This place is small. This place is one small room with a bed by the wall that is just a blue foam mat on a metal surface, like the mats for PE when she was at school. The smell in the room is ugly, of sick and poo and cleaning fluid. There are shiny white tiles on the walls like bricks. A line of orange tiles runs through them halfway up. Voices go past and doors bang outside. Sludgy noise thickening the air, on and off. Gloria thinks to scream and cry to block things out, but it won't work. Everything is bad, but this room is empty. And people are moving slowly and talking slow and nice like nothing is wrong. Before she goes into this small room people are talking slow and nice to her. Another lady police says What's your name and Tyrone tells her Gloria's name and she says Oh Gloria, that's a nice name, reminds me of that old song. And then she sings Gloria, Gloria! at her, and she smiles. And she asks Tyrone Does she have any medical conditions? Has she taken anything? Has she had any head injuries? And she asks Tyrone all lots of other questions.

She says, 'You're going to stay in a cell for a bit, Gloria, while we get ready to ask you questions. It's just like a small room with a bed in it.'

'Do I go with her?' Tyrone says.

'No, she'll need to go on her own for this bit, sorry,' the lady says, and she smiles at Gloria and at Tyrone. She says, 'It's just procedure. We'll keep an eye on her though.'

'I'll be out here Gloria,' Tyrone says, 'I ain't going nowhere, okay?'

The room is small. Gloria can see all the entrances and exits because there is only one and it's a big metal door and she can see it from wherever she is in the room. So no one can come in that she won't know about. And there are small squares of twisted glass up high in the wall but outside them is all dark. And you couldn't get in or out of them anyway, it's not a proper window, there is only the door. The door is closed. It don't look like a normal door. It has a hole in it to look through that can open or close, and the hole is closed, covered over with more metal so she can't see outside it.

The police still didn't hit her yet like they hit Jack. Maybe she will go to court and go to prison and they won't even hit her.

They took the handcuffs off. Her arms feel like they are floating. Police tell her to take off her coat and her shoes and she does, and they take them. And they take her blue furry purse and they keep it. So now she has no shoes on. Her shoes are all wet anyway. Her socks are still wet even without them. Her trousers are wet where she's been on the ground. A police holds her hand and puts her fingers on a screen on a computer machine. Tyrone watches. And they tell her to open her mouth so they can touch inside with a cotton bud. Tyrone nods and says Open your mouth Gloria, so she does. And they put a cotton bud in her mouth and take it out of her mouth again quite soon after. Tyrone says Be cool Gloria, just be calm. He says it worried, like it's urgent. Like he's frightened. She can tell it's important so she tries hard, the panic stiff in her chest, and she keeps it there, all tight and balled up and she don't let it out. She puts her fingers where they show her and opens her mouth. They take a photo and she tries to smile for it but she don't feel like smiling. She can't make it happen. And everybody speaks quiet and calm and they smile at her and say Well done Gloria you're doing really well. Being arrested is getting in trouble and the police catch bad people but everyone is talking to Gloria all nice like she ain't in any trouble and she ain't done nothing bad.

But she pushed the man. And they know. Even though Tyrone keeps saying to them This is a big mistake and You got this all wrong. And he says You can ask her questions but she ain't gonna talk to you. She don't talk a lot. She barely even talks to me. And they are calm and speak nice and have tight smiles and say Let's just get this over and done with sir, shall we? Because Gloria pushes the man and he hits on the car and he falls on the road, and he ain't Jack, and they know.

She pushed him I seen the whole thing she pushed him.
It weren't your fault mate she pushed him.
Hey! Hey!

Gloria sits on the bed. She wriggles in hard against the wall so her back is against the wall and she can feel it pressing in on her. Her body folds in tight in to fit the corner where the bed and the wall join. She moves her arms apart and hits them on the wall on either side, bouncing them forwards and back, just to feel that she can. The cold tile is raw on her cold hands. She watches the door. So I can keep an eye. She thinks of Jack beside her, both of them sitting on his bed with their backs pressed against the wall like it's a sofa. Jack quiet, his breathing gentle and soft. Right before. Before. I got a feeling, Gloria, he says. I got a feeling like this is the last we gonna see of each other.

She can smell him. The spice of his sweat, the petrol smell of his drink, the brown smell of his smoke. She can smell him in this room hot among the cold dirty scents. He is here somewhere. Outside this door. He will open the hole and look at her. All the feeling in her chest is big and tight and she ain't got room to breathe. And if she screams Jack will come in and press her on the blue mattress and say Shut up shut up. She tries to breathe and it's little and shaky and not enough and she does it more and more because the air is so thick with smell, the smell of Jack and the smells of sick and cleaner, it's too thick to breathe. The air won't come inside her lungs properly. She tries and tries but she can only get a little bit at a time. Her ankle is sore. Her lips are sore from where the boy presses on her mouth. She closes her eyes to stop the shiny white tiles glaring at her. The boy is there. When she closes her eyes the boy comes with the knife and he is in front of her face and rain is dripping on him. I will hurt you I will cut you keep your mouth shut. She opens her eyes but the feeling is still there, the trapped tight feeling bursting her. And even Tyrone telling her to keep her mouth shut, he says it nicely Be cool stay still be calm but he means Shut up Gloria shut up! He means Don't scream and make noise to show what you're feeling don't smash your fists don't rock don't bite yourself be cool.

Gloria pulls her legs up tight, her knees to her chest. She wraps her arms around them and holds herself in tight. Tight against the bed and the wall. She bites her arm through her damp black jumper. It tastes of wet and rain. It hurts. She digs her teeth and feels the pinch of her flesh shifting against the bone. Her teeth feel warm and safe. A good feeling in her mouth and a bad feeling in her arm. She holds them together inside herself. Soft and warm and hard and sharp. The boy ran away. The boy runs away and maybe they caught him and maybe he's in here too somewhere in another room. She can smell him too. Rain and washing powder and old sweat and weed. Maybe they hit him like they hit Jack. She thinks of Jack get hit. Jack scream his noise into the pavement. Jack screw up his eyes and shout out. His tears touch onto the cement and dry away. She stays solid and tight. Holding herself tight. Making sure the feelings stay inside.

After a long time the hole in the door slides open. Blue eyes are looking at her, the same plastic blue like Jack's eyes. It's Jack. He is watching her. She ain't made noise. She's kept still and quiet. There is a clank clunk sound and the metal door opens.

A lady police is standing there watching her. There are noises coming from the corridor behind her. Voices in the distance, a metal door slamming. Gloria looks to see if anyone's standing behind the lady, but Jack ain't there.

'Gloria,' the lady says. 'Do you want to come with me now? We're gonna go to another room and ask you some questions. Tyrone will be there.' She is still talking nice and quiet and slow, like Gloria ain't in trouble. 'Come with me,' she says.

Gloria stays where she is, sitting on the metal bed all pressed in tight. Then she gets up and stands up. Her legs are numb. Her ankle hurts and she falls a little bit. She steps sideways, catching herself. The lady police stands in the door waiting for her. Gloria walks over to her. Gloria must be very cold because she is shaking. The woman gestures for her to go in front.

Outside of the room it is a corridor with lots of other

metal doors all along it with big handles on them. The doors are closed. There is a man shouting behind one of them. It is a different language and Gloria don't understand.

'We're going that way,' the woman says. She points along the corridor. 'Go on,' she says.

Gloria walks. Some of the holes in the other metal doors are open. She can see inside small rooms like the one she was just in. Some of the doors have the holes closed. The lady police is walking right behind. Gloria can hear the lady's trousers swishing and the man's voice shouting. A man is coming towards her with a police right behind him. They walk past and the police opens one of the metal doors for him to go inside.

'Down here,' the lady says to Gloria, pointing. They walk along another corridor. Police walk past them. Two men walk past.

The lady points towards an open door. It is a normal door made of wood. 'In there, Gloria,' says the lady.

Tyrone is sitting inside the room. He stands up when he sees Gloria coming in. 'You okay Gloria, yeah?' he says.

There is a table and chairs. Tyrone is by one chair. There is a man sitting in another chair.

'Sit down, Gloria,' the lady says, and she points at the chair next to Tyrone. Gloria sits. She pulls her chair closer into the table. Chair legs squeak and scrape on the floor. She pulls the chair in closer and closer. More scraping noise. The table presses on her tummy and she feels all wrapped in. She pushes her ankles behind the legs of the chair and twists them around. It hurts where her ankle is sore but she does it anyway. She wants to feel the table pressing in on her front and the back of the chair pressing in on her back and the chair legs pressing in on her legs. So she can feel where everything is and where she ends.

The man talks. He says his name. 'We need to ask you some questions about things that happened this evening,' he says. 'Gloria, we're trying to make this as quick as possible cos we know it's difficult for you. We want to make this take as short a time as possible. Now you have Tyrone here as your appropriate adult. We're gonna record this interview so we have a record of what was said.'

Gloria breathes in hard to feel the table pressing against her more. She rocks a tiny bit so she feels the back of the chair behind her and the edge of the table in front of her, and it makes the room move. It's very bright in the room. All the faces look too close, the two police and Tyrone's, all their voices come at her hard and fast and loud. The light bounces on their foreheads and cheeks at weird angles, casting sharp shadows on their eyes and chins. When the man speaks his face looks like moving triangles and jagged shapes of skin.

'Do you understand?' the man says.

Tyrone and the man and the lady look at her. Faces bright and close together, nonsense patterns of eyes and teeth.

'Yes,' Gloria says.

'This is ridiculous,' Tyrone says. 'Ain't you lot got better things you could be doing?'

'Yeah. Plenty,' the lady police says. She looks at Tyrone. He looks back at her. She don't smile.

'If we could just get on with this,' the man says.

Tyrone sighs and rubs his hands on his face.

There is a machine on the table with a little blue screen on it. The man presses a button on the screen. He says things. He says his name and the lady's name. He asks Gloria to say her own name but she don't say it because he already knows what her name is and she don't know why he is asking again. He says her name. He tells Tyrone to say his name and Tyrone says his name. He says the TV words again that the lady says in the car. He has a pad of paper and a pen on the table in front of him. He writes something down on the paper. He says, 'Fifth November 2017, Manor Park Police Station, interview commenced at twenty-two forty-nine.'

'Gloria,' the lady says, her mouth flickering as she speaks, shadows stretching across her cheeks. 'Can you tell me what you were doing today, this evening?'

Today this evening. Gloria don't know how to say everything that happened this evening.

'We know you got on the bus with your housemates and your carers, is that right?'

Isatright isatright.

This is like before. Sitting here in the room and getting questions asked about what happens. It's a long time ago. And Gloria and Mum come to a police station and they go in a room and it's like this room. And Mum sits beside her like Tyrone is and police ask her questions. There are chairs and a table and they press a button to record everything what she says.

'Gloria, you were on the bus. Did anything happen on the bus?'

Do you know this man? They show her a picture of Jack. Did you meet him before?

Gloria, Mum says. You gotta answer them darling, it's important.

They show her the picture of Jack. They put it on the table. Gloria looks at it. In the picture Jack isn't smiling. He is caught, frowning slightly, his mouth a tiny bit open like he is just about to say something. He has a cut on his head and around his eye is bruised.

'We're doing everything we can to make this as easy as possible for you, Gloria. But we need you to talk to us.'

Do you know him? the man says. And she nods yes.

'On the bus. This evening. Gloria?'

How do you know him? Did you used to meet him, spend time with him?

Yes.

What did you used to do? Where would you go?

Talk.

His flat.

Did he ever hurt you, Gloria?

Never once. Never once put my hands on you.

'You got off the bus, didn't you, Gloria?'

Gloria nods.

How did you meet him? How long have you known him?

Did he buy you things?

Chips.

And did he – did he ever do anything? To make you feel uncomfortable?

'Did you meet anyone? When you got off the bus?'

Okay. Let's go back to the night of August the eleventh. Or the day, really. Can you tell us what you and Jack had been doing that day?

'It's really important that you answer these questions, Gloria.'

And how was he? Did he seem cross, or angry, or upset?

'She ain't gonna speak,' Tyrone says.

The police holds up his hand. 'Please sir, can you not interrupt,' he says.

Can you remember anything from that day?

Could you tell me about it?

'Did you see a man, Gloria? A man when you got off the bus?'

You were with him for quite a long time that day, weren't you? Till quite late?

You didn't normally stay out with him that late.

'Did you talk to anyone?'

Can you tell us where you were? What you were doing?

His place.

And what were you doing?

'Gloria, people have said they saw you. They saw you

push a man. You pushed a man and he fell into the road, Gloria. He hit a car. Can you tell me if that's true?'

Gloria, you're not in any trouble. You've seen some important things and we need to know all about them. The more you can tell us, the more helpful it is.

Do you know this man?

And they show a picture. Another picture. A picture of the man Jack hurt. The man who stopped his car. The picture is of the man in a garden in the sunshine. He is wearing a black T-shirt. It looks warm. He is smiling. He looks happy in the picture.

His name is Usman Miah. Mr Miah. Do you know him?

'Did you push anyone? Did you push a man, Gloria?'

Okay. Can you tell us what happened? That evening. Can you tell us what you saw?

'It's really important you answer these questions, Gloria. Even just a simple yes or no. So we can find out what happened.'

You were outside, weren't you? Outside Jack's house. Where were you going?

Home.

'Where were you going when you got off the bus, Gloria?'

Good. You were going home. And what happened then?

The car stops. There's a man in the car. He says You okay?

That's great, Gloria. And what happened then? What did the man do next?

He gets out the car.

Gloria you're doing so well, answering all these questions.

'Gloria, we really need you to speak to us.'

Hands on ears. She puts her hands on her ears and presses in on her head.

'Gloria,' the lady says. 'I know this is difficult. You've had a long day. We just need to hear about what happened. Okay? What happened when you got off the bus? Did you see a man?'

Gloria is quiet. Listening to the questions inside her head. She takes her hands off her ears.

'Did you—' the police says.

Gloria interrupts her.

'Jack hit him,' Gloria says.

The two police look at each other. 'Who's Jack?' the man says. He looks at Tyrone. Tyrone shrugs and shakes his head.

'Gloria?' Tyrone says. 'Who's Jack?'

Gloria don't speak.

'Could be anyone,' Tyrone says. 'Could be something from a TV show she's seen, anything.'

'Who did Jack hit?' the lady says. 'What did Jack do? Gloria?'

Gloria looks at them. She's got it wrong. The answer. She ain't told them right. The last time she had more goes. She comes back to the police station again with her mum and they ask her more questions. She gets to try again and again and tell the words better.

11

White tiles on the walls. Shiny white tiles. A line of faded orange tiles halfway up, going all the way round. There are black lines in between the tiles. The tiles are smooth and the black lines are gritty and grainy. There are cracks and lines on the tiles but she can't feel them when she runs her fingernails over them, even pressing very hard, even going slowly. There is no bump or jag. Fingernails glide along over the smooth white then scrape over the grainy black, along and down, following the narrow line, then sail over smooth white again.

'Will Jack say sorry?' Gloria says one time to Mum. They are at home. They are at home after the police station and Mum is cross. Gloria is sitting on the sofa and Mum is standing up.

Mum looks at her and frowns, opens her mouth to speak and stops like she don't know what to say. Like she's cross at the question. Then she says, 'It don't matter if he's sorry. Some things are too big for sorry, Gloria.'

'Why you worrying about Jack?' she says. 'Jack done a really bad thing. Jack killed that man, that Mr Miah. You know that Gloria? What you worrying about Jack for? Who cares if he's gonna say sorry?'

Gloria don't speak.

'That man had a family,' Mum says. 'He had a wife and kids. You think they care if Jack's gonna say sorry?'

The tips of Gloria's fingers squish into the gap where two tiles end. Her hand is all purple with old marks where she been biting it. Her teeth dig into her other hand. She deepens in and squeezes with her mouth, feeling the pain and pressure neat and new. It keeps her together, one long loop of her, feelings changing as they meet at her mouth and her skin. She's frighten. Everything is in her chest pounding and clawing. The Coke from earlier. Coke coming up her throat, tasting like summer. Someone is shouting outside. A man's voice. Shouting and screaming. Gloria bites harder. She pushes her other hand on her ear. She still can hear the screaming noise. She sits down on the blue bed and curls her knees up. She stops biting and puts both hands on her ears and presses hard. The noise dims. She looks at the shiny tiles, yellow light running along them. It reminds her of the swimming pool when she was a kid. When she used to go on trips.

They ask her questions and she told it wrong. Is she gonna stay here forever? She's in prison. Is she gonna stay here because she hit the man? Stay here for a long long time.

When Jack killed that Mr Miah the police put him away inside a van and drove him away. They put Gloria inside a car and drive her away too. They drive her to her house. A man police walks with her to the door and knocks on the door even though Gloria has a key. Mum opens the door and her hands go on Gloria, her hands pull Gloria inside. The man police and Mum are talking in the living room. His voice is wrong in the house. There's blood on Gloria's shoes. Gloria kicks off her shoes, one after the other, she's scared to touch them cos of the blood. There's flakes of dried red blood coming off them, onto the fake wood lino. Gloria kicks her shoes away against the wall, she kicks them hard, she wants them to go right into the wall and disappear, she don't want to see them no more. Her bra hurts round her chest. Her clothes feel tight and sticky. Her clothes are dirty. They were there with her on the street. She pulls off her T-shirt and bra and pedal pushers and pants and drops them on the floor and kicks them. She bites her arm hard. She presses her head and it ain't enough and she pulls her own hair tight, to feel all how tight her head is and nothing can get in. She hits her head.

'Gloria,' Mum says. 'Gloria.'

Mum is standing with the police. Mum is wearing clothes. The police is wearing clothes, thick black vest keeping him separate from the world. Gloria bites in her arm.

'Upstairs,' Mum says. She pushes Gloria up onto the steps. The police goes. Door open and close.

Mum puts hands on Gloria's shoulders and pushes her upstairs. She holds Gloria's arm away from her mouth so she can't bite. Gloria walks away from her shoes and clothes and away from the flakes of blood. Mum pushes Gloria into the bathroom. She pulls the light on. The bathroom is shiny and creamy white. The taps shine. The fan buzzes. An insect taps against the window.

'Clean your teeth Glor,' Mum says, like it's an ordinary night. Like she can go bed and sleep. Mum gets Gloria's toothbrush and puts toothpaste on it. She offers it to Gloria. 'You'll feel better,' she says.

Gloria stands still. The mat is soft under her feet. She scrunches her toes in it and the mat wrinkles up. She can't do normal things. Mum points the toothbrush at her. Mum's hand is shaking, the shine on the toothpaste wobbling. Gloria don't move. Mum puts Gloria's toothbrush down on the sink and puts her hand on Gloria's shoulder and they go together, moving to Gloria's bedroom. Mum don't try to make her do normal things no more. Gloria don't get ready for bed. She just lies straight down in the dark. Mum pulls the duvet over her. The duvet smells of washing power and of Gloria and of smoke a little bit, from where Jack's smoke has caught in her hair. She pushes it off.

Mum goes to the chest of drawers and turns on Gloria's special lamp. Orange, blue, green and pink light turns round the room in circles. Gloria watches it on the ceiling. Blue chasing orange. Pink chasing green. Then round again.

Mum lays down on the bed beside her. She rubs Gloria's shoulder, then she takes her hand away.

'Gloria,' Mum says. A tight whisper. Gloria don't speak. Mum don't speak either. Mum lets silence happen. They lie together on the bed. The coloured lights spin over the ceiling and the walls. Gloria looks at it but she keeps seeing the man on the ground, the blood all over. Police and Jack. She cries. She does it quiet. It's easier to do it quiet now. She ain't got the energy to make noise, her throat and lungs can't do it. So she does it not calling out to no one. Just quiet so no one knows. But Mum is there still. Mum puts her hand on Gloria's back. Gloria's curled up and Mum's curled up too, fitting around her. Gloria can feel the warmth of her, all along her back, breathing soft all night while Gloria cries quiet.

The daylight comes early, bright grey, drowning out the colours of Gloria's lamp. Both of them are still lying there. Gloria never sleeps all night. When she turns to look at Mum, Mum's eyes are open, watching her. Mum says, 'Morning babe.'

12

They let her out.

They give her back her coat and shoes, and her blue furry purse. She squeezes it and feels the shape of her money and lighter inside. She wedges her feet into her cold damp shoes. The broken-sole trainer is wetter than the other one. It squelches water around her foot when she walks.

The lady police takes her to where Tyrone is. He is sitting on a chair, slumped sideways, yawning. He stands up when he sees her. 'Come on then Gloria,' he says.

The police is talking to her, and Tyrone is listening and nodding, and Gloria can't get her coat done up. The long bit on the bottom won't go into the zip properly and she can't make it come up. She tries and tries and pulls it and it won't go. She leaves it open.

She don't get why they're letting her go. She's meant to

be in trouble. She pushed a man and he ain't Jack, and she never answered any of the questions. Maybe they should keep her shoes. Maybe they should hit her.

'Let's go,' Tyrone says. He puts a hand on her shoulder. She walks with him across the cracked grey floor. There are lots of people standing around. There is a man with a bandage on his head. There is a man and a woman arguing. I'm not being funny mate but I never fucking done nothing so why you— Nobody stops Gloria. Nobody shouts at her or tells her to say sorry.

They go out through the glass doors, into the night. Outside it's cold. The chill hits into her through her open coat. It's stopped raining but the pavement and the roads are still wet. The panic that is stiff inside her chest spreads away and turns into hollow and heartbeat and shaking, and she wants to cry and sit down. All the cars rush by, the white and orange and red lights spinning and sparkling on the black tarmac.

'Freedom,' Tyrone says. He looks at her. She don't say nothing. Tyrone gets his phone out his pocket and touches the screen. 'Getting a cab,' he says. 'What a night, eh Gloria?' He shakes his head.

In the distance she hears bangs and thuds of fireworks. She looks but she can't see them in the sky. They must be behind buildings.

'Unbelievable,' Tyrone says. 'Unbelievable them taking you in like that. Nicking you. Ridiculous.'

'Going home?' Gloria says.

'Yeah,' Tyrone nods. 'Home. I'm knackered,' he says. 'Bet you're exhausted.'

A red bus pulls up at the bus stop and a man gets off and walks away down the road. Gloria looks up at the heavy orange sky.

Where were you going when you got off the bus?

'You okay?' Tyrone says.

Everything is in her head all jumbled up and she don't know what's happening. 'Am I going prison?' she says.

'Prison?' Tyrone says. 'No, you're not going prison, Gloria. You didn't do nothing. You're going home. Police bail.'

She is quiet. Because she did do something. She pushed the man.

They wait. Tyrone puts his hands in his pockets. Gloria starts to shiver. She pulls her coat closed and holds it tight around her to try and keep the cold out.

A car pulls up. Headlights. 'This is us,' Tyrone says.

He walks towards the car, then he turns round and waits for her to follow. He opens the back door for her. She slides in and Tyrone gets in after her. Inside the car it's warmer. Music is playing.

'Alright?' Tyrone says to the driver.

'Yes boss. Greengate Lodge?' says the driver.

'That's right,' Tyrone says.

Gloria lifts her wrists apart and together, a clapping motion. It don't make the same sound with her wrists as it does when she claps with her hands. She looks out the window at the cars and streets rolling by, the lights from shopfronts, red and blue letters glowing in the darkness. She can't read any of them, the car is moving too fast. They are gone before she can work out what they say.

There is a group of boys letting off fireworks on the corner. The boys flit around, hooded figures silhouetted against the white and blue sparks. The cab jerks to a stop as a firework streaks across the road, a dazzling trail. Gloria is pushed forwards.

'Fucking idiots,' the driver says to Tyrone, waving his hand at the fireworks and the kids.

Tyrone shakes his head. 'Every year,' he says.

'Not just Guy Fawkes,' the driver says. 'Eid, Diwali, New Year's. Acting like idiots. So dangerous, you know?'

The firework clamours and sparkles in the gutter, throwing pieces of blue and white light onto the street. The car starts moving again. Gloria twists around to keep looking back at the firework. The sparks are getting less, changing to dull yellow light.

Tyrone gets out his phone and puts it to his ear. 'Alright Sharifah?' he says. 'Put the kettle on love. We're on our way back. Getting a cab. Yeah. Yeah, she seems okay. Quiet. Bit freaked out I think. I know, it's unbelievable. I want time and a half for this, I tell you. Yeah. Yeah. Alright, in a bit. Soon.'

He ends the call. He shakes his head and looks out the window. Gloria can't see the firework no more. She turns around again, facing forwards. She listens to the music and rocks to make the night move the way she wants it to.

Sharifah is waiting for them. She is standing in the doorway of the office, watching as they come in. 'Gloria,' she says. She looks at Gloria and shakes her head.

Tyrone unzips his coat. It makes a sweet continuous crunching noise as the zip sweeps down. Gloria turns her head to look. The black puffy fabric of his coat comes apart, his grey jumper showing through the widening gap.

'I need to talk to you about what's happened today,' Sharifah says to Gloria. 'But I just wanna speak with Tyrone first, on our own. Okay? Will you give us a minute, Gloria?'

Gloria nods.

'Thank you,' Sharifah says. She looks at Tyrone. He raises his eyebrows at her. They go into the office together and close the door.

Gloria stands there looking at the closed door. Her feet are cold and wet. She kicks her shoes off, scraping and scraping the toe of one shoe on the heel of the other until they pop off and lie vacant in the hall. Her socks are damp too. She sits down on the floor and pulls them off, first one foot then the other. Her feet are cold and dead. They tingle in the air, free of the damp fabric. She balls each sock and tucks them into her shoes. She pushes her shoes against the wall because Sharifah always calls out Who's left their shoes in the middle of the corridor? Gloria!

Gloria waits for Sharifah. Through the open living room door she can see Haider and Suzanne watching TV, the backs of their heads above the sofa. But she don't go in. She wants quiet.

After a while Sharifah opens the office door again. 'Gloria,' she says. 'Can I talk to you now, is that okay? Can you come in?'

Come with me. We're going that way. Gloria has had enough of people bossing her through doors, but she goes in. Sharifah closes the door. Tyrone is sitting on a chair, leaning back, swivelling it a little side to side. He is holding a mug of tea.

'Sit down,' Sharifah says.

Sit down Gloria.

No.

Gloria stays standing up. Sharifah shrugs. 'Okay, you don't have to sit down,' she says.

Sharifah sits down. She looks at Gloria. Gloria looks at the desk. There is a kettle in the corner with a box of teabags and a carton of milk and a green mug. There are piles of paper, and folders, green and red and blue. There is a computer. The computer screen is glowing blue-white. There is writing hovering on the screen.

'How are you feeling Gloria?' Sharifah says. 'You okay?'

Gloria don't say nothing.

'You're not wearing shoes,' Sharifah says.

Gloria don't speak.

Sharifah looks at Gloria's feet. She is biting her lip like she's thinking about what to say. 'I know what happened with the police. I know they arrested you,' she says eventually. She waits a moment. 'That must have been scary,' she says.

Next to her, Tyrone drains his mug. He reaches across and puts it on the desk. Gloria thinks about the man she pushed. His body twisting on the road. She thinks of the boy and the knife.

'I don't want you to worry too much about the police,' Sharifah says. 'I know it was scary. It was a mistake. I think it must be cos you look like someone else. Someone who has done something.' Sharifah looks over at Tyrone and then back at Gloria. 'But they'll investigate properly, okay?' she continues. 'They'll look into everything what happened, they'll look at the CCTV. It'll all get sorted. It should never of happened. I'm gonna speak to your social worker in the morning and – well. You don't need to know all that. But we're gonna sort it out, okay Gloria?'

Luh kinto everything luh kinto.

Gloria thinks of the man who ain't Jack. The back of his head, the anger in his shoulders as he walks along. His hands cupped in front of him, rolling a cigarette. The tingling in her palms as her hands slam into him.

'Sorry,' Gloria says.

'Sorry?' Sharifah says. 'What you sorry for Gloria? Sorry for running away? You shouldn't of run away, but we can talk about it later. Tomorrow. It's—'

'Sorry I pushed the man,' Gloria says.

There is quiet. Sharifah and Tyrone look at each other.

Tyrone leans forward. 'Gloria,' he says, 'no one thinks you done that. I know the police said it, but they have to ask you. It's their job. It don't mean you done it.'

Gloria don't speak.

'Did you...' Sharifah says. Then she stops.

'Sorry,' Gloria says.

'Gloria,' Tyrone says. 'You didn't push no one, okay? We know that. So don't say sorry, alright?' He looks at Sharifah, and she looks back at him. 'Don't say it again,' he says. 'Don't say it to nobody, okay? I know normally it's good to say sorry, and it makes things better. But this time, don't – don't say sorry. Okay? Just don't...' He breaks off. He rubs his hands over his face.

Some things are too big for sorry, Gloria.

'Gloria,' Sharifah says. 'This is important. We know you didn't push no one. It's good to say sorry. But sometimes if you say sorry for things that aren't your fault, it – people get confused.' She stops talking. She looks at Tyrone again.

'I pushed a man,' Gloria says.

'No you didn't,' Sharifah says. 'The police – the police have got confused. They think you are – you look like someone who pushed a man. They'll investigate. Check the cameras and that. They'll see it weren't you.'

Gloria don't know what to do. Hands on ears, bite arm, shout, scream. She don't know how to make them understand. The police know. She wants to say sorry. She did do something wrong. She stands looking at Sharifah, her mouth open. Not talking.

'Gloria,' Tyrone says. He leans forward. 'The police was wrong, okay? They should never of arrested you. They got it wrong. They did something wrong. You don't need to say sorry. The police should say sorry. They should say sorry to you. You didn't do nothing.'

She stands there. She stares at Tyrone, at Sharifah. They both look back at her, their eyes wide and sincere. She scans the room, the white walls, the noticeboard cluttered with papers, the calendar showing 2017. Her eyes rest on the clock on the wall. She sees the big hand move, jumping forward. It startles her.

Tyrone and Sharifah are both watching her, waiting for her to speak. She don't know what to say. She did push him. She hurt him. She wants to say sorry.

'You can't let yourself get in trouble for something you didn't do,' Tyrone says.

Gloria shakes her head.

'You've got confused,' Sharifah says gently. 'People have been asking you if you did something and treating you as though you did it, so you think you did it. But you didn't do it.'

Sharifah looks at Gloria. Gloria looks at the desk. She runs her tongue on the inside of her teeth, moving it fast and invisible while the rest of her stays still. She looks at the green folder, the corner of it just hanging over the edge of the desk. Sharifah and Tyrone look at each other.

'Gloria,' Tyrone says. 'What did you do when you got off of the bus?'

Tyrone leaves a long piece of quiet. Gloria waits. Sharifah and Tyrone are both looking at her now, wanting to hear her answer. She thinks of the man on the street in front of her, her memories crowding in, the need to hurt making pressure in her hands. She shakes her head.

'Sorry,' she says again.

'Okay,' Sharifah says. She sounds unsure. 'Okay, Gloria. It's been a long day, innit. A really long day. You must be tired. Tyrone's tired. I'm tired. Why don't we all sleep on it, hmm? Why don't we talk about this in the morning?'

Sharifah looks at Gloria. Gloria keeps on looking at the green folder. Sharifah looks at Tyrone. He nods.

'Tyrone needs to go home,' Sharifah says. 'I need to go to bed. You need to go to bed.'

Gloria stays where she is.

'Come on,' Sharifah says. 'Let's not have any more drama tonight, eh?'

13

In her room she hits the wall. Hard. Her hand hurts too much. Her hand has all marks on it and now her hand is swelling and sore and the wall is still there. No mark on the wall. The wall is white but not shiny. It's rough paint and it has lots of grey tiny shadows all over it. Not like the room she was in before. Small. A bed that is just a blue foam mat on a metal surface. Gloria sitting on the metal bed, pressed in tight to the corner between the bed and the wall. Gloria pressing on the white tile walls.

Her duvet is yellow. She grabs and pulls, trying to rip it. The fabric don't break. The fabric feels sharp on her hands because she's pulling it so tight. Her hands want to cry. She grabs the duvet and bunches it and pushes it and throws it off the bed. She grabs the white sheet off the bed and throws it after the duvet. The sheet has elastic in the corners and it curls up and floats down, air sinking out of it. Yellow and white over the floor. Gloria throws the pillow. It hits the wall and lands in the pile of her bedding. She kneels on the bare mattress. She smacks at the mattress. Her fist bounces off.

She wants to make the room bad.

The mattress is heavy and hard to move. She shoves at it with her hip, moving hard, her whole body. The mattress tips and bends. It twists sideways on the bed then slides at an angle to the floor. Lands on top of the white and yellow sheet and duvet. The wood of the bed is exposed. Grey dust where the bed meets the wall. Wooden slats digging into her hands and thighs. Gloria don't care. The room don't make sense. The bed don't make sense, broken like this. Split into mattress and frame. The whole room looks different. The bed don't look like a bed no more. Good. She wants the room bad.

She goes to where her coat is hanging on the back of the door. She reaches into its pocket, pulls out her blue furry purse and takes out her new lighter. She clicks it and nothing happens. She tries again. An orange flame comes. The flame flickers and moves and bends. The flame is bright blue at the bottom. It hurts the skin of her thumb keeping it alive.

She grabs the duvet and presses it on the flame to make the duvet go on fire, to make the room burn. She holds it there. The flame goes away. She clicks the lighter again with her sore thumb but the flame won't come. She throws the lighter. It cracks against her chest of drawers.

She stamps on the mattress. She jumps and flings herself down, landing like the man did. Falling forward. Try to move his legs to catch up. He trips. Gloria falls forward. She hits her head on the wood frame bed, hard. She cries. She goes still. She don't make noise or sob. Her eyes just water from the pain. She don't wipe her eyes. She lifts her hand to her head like the man did, touching to see how much hurt there is.

She lies there. The ceiling looks high above her. The white light shining inside the cream-coloured lampshade. She stares at it and her tears make the light spike out. She remembers her bed at Mum's house. The coloured lamp at night. Waking in the morning for college. Waking up to go to Jack's house.

The bed at Jack's house. Duvet half off. Gloria lying on the bed with Jack holding her there so she can't move. Gloria sitting on the bed. Jack beside her. Jack by the window looking at the sunset. Beautiful, this.

Outside there's a bang like an explosion.

Another bang and a flash of light.

She goes to the window and pulls the white curtain back. She presses her face against the glass to block out the reflection of her room. She can see the trees moving in the wind, the dark square of grass. There are people in the park. Dark figures, darker patches moving. Shouts and laughing. Men's voices. Phone torches come on and off, white lights weaving around in the grass. A little orange light shoots up into the sky and then bursts open in purple and white sparks.

Her breath steams on the glass. Her lips press against it, cold. She pushes her fingers into the reflection of her bedroom, the bed swirled in a mess on the floor. She wants to break the whole room, smash out of it.

She's not confused. She knows what she did. She pushes a man, she runs away, she finds a place inside trees. She don't want this little room. Yellow light, a small box in a big city, hard white walls keeping everything inside. The night shut out. In her head there's somewhere else. Somewhere cold and derelict. Somewhere by a river. A little fire. A hole outside for the toilet.

But she don't want Jack. She don't want Jack's flat or Jack's room by the river or Jack's walk in the park. She don't want Jack beside her, holding her arm, saying She's fine and saying Shut up Gloria. The feel of his sweat and his breath beside her. Him shouting and hurting. She don't want Jack. She don't want to see him. If she sees him again she'll push him, she'll shove him, she'll make him run away.

Gloria reaches for the window. She sees her own face coming towards her in the glass, her arm reaching out. She grabs the handle and opens the window. She leans out into the cold night, out through the reflection of her room. Somebody calls out something she can't understand and then there is fizzing and a whoosh as a golden spark flies up into the sky and then another then another and another. The sparks burst open, red and green and blue. More and more fireworks, big and dripping, falling down like they will land on her and set the trees on fire. Everything is lit up. The trees and the group of men standing in the middle of the park, dark figures in the grass, moving and shifting. A boy on a bike turning loops, a darker patch of night going in circles. She don't know if it's a dream. Maybe she will wake up and all of it didn't happen, pushing the man and the boy holding her, showing her the knife. She will wake up back in her bed with the mattress back in the right place and everything will be all the same. Jack will still be in prison. But the night air is cold on her face and neck and it feels like she's awake. It feels like everything is real.

She pushes out of the window. She pushes out so she's leaning out. Fireworks bright above her smashing open. Boom bang across the park. The window frame is digging in her hips. She's shivering in her T-shirt. The night is cold on her skin. She can see over the park where she sat with Jack, the bench all lit up in flashes. All small below her. Men in the grass small below her. It smells of smoke. Not like Jack smoking but proper smoke, like everything burning up and blowing away. She pulls hard on the white plastic window frame and climbs her knees up onto the windowsill. Her bare feet sliding on the windowsill. She sits and pushes her legs out the window. All of her inside the night. Her back can still feel the warmth and light of her room but the rest of her is out in the night, floating high above the park, watching the benches and the paths and the fountain and the fireworks smashing the sky to pieces up above. She feels like she could take the night and hold it. She could hurt herself. She could lean forward now and hurtle herself down past the trees to the hard ground. She could break on the ground like the fireworks are breaking in the sky.

Gloria leans forward. One hand on the window frame. The corner of it gripping into her hand, hurting the skin. One hand feeling out into the cold air. The men are looking now. They gather, a shifting pool in the middle of the park, flashes of white phone light rippling off them. The sky smoky orange. She leans herself further into the night. One hand holding tight to the warm yellow room, the little safe box. The rest of her pulling out into the darkness.

Her hand slips on the window.

She tips forward.

Men shout.

The sky is not there. Her face gasps and there's treetops and phone lights and shouting. She jerks and pulls backwards and flails her arms and her hand catches hard, grips hard. Hand holds hard cold plastic. The window frame hurting her fingers. She's pressed sideways. Pressed against the window. Her hand holding the window hard, her arm hugging it, side of her bum digging in, her legs hanging off into air, her head facing down. The men are shouting.

She holds on. She's shaking all over. She wriggles herself backwards. Tips the weight of herself backwards. Tumbles herself away from the night and into her warm bright room. Onto the grey carpet.

She lies beside her broken bed. She takes the yellow duvet and pulls it over her, rubs her face into it so everything's dark and warm and covered up.

14

Gloria chooses the card with blue and red colours because the man looks like Jack and Jack likes that football team. She takes it to the man at the counter. 'Two pound fifty dear,' he says.

Gloria gives him a five-pound note. Five-pound notes are a nice colour, blue-green like the sea. She don't like giving them away for things. The man takes the note and he gives her two gold-and-silver pound coins and two silver twenty p coins and lots of little brown penny coins. The money feels dirty in her hand. She puts the money in her blue fluffy purse and puts it back in her pocket. She wipes her hand hard on her trousers. She can still smell the money smell on her hand all metal. Her hand feels dry from it.

She goes back home. In her room she opens the card and writes her name in it. Gloria. She folds it closed and puts it in the envelope. She licks the envelope. It tastes like sweets. She presses it shut.

Downstairs, Tyrone is in the living room. He's on the sofa with Haider and Suzanne. He's looking at his phone. Haider and Suzanne are looking at the telly.

Gloria gives Tyrone the card. He looks up from his phone. She's holding the white envelope out to him. 'You want me to take this?' he says. She pushes it at him. He takes it. 'For me?' he says. 'Thank you, Gloria.' He goes to open it.

'No,' she says.

'Not for me?' He's watching her, his eyes looking at her.

'Not you,' she says.

'Who's it for? You want me to give it to someone?'

'The man,' she says.

He tips his head to one side, rests his cheek on his fist. 'What man? Now you got a man Gloria? You dark horse. They say it's the quiet ones you have to watch.'

'For the man,' Gloria says.

'What man?' he says again.

'I pushed the man,' Gloria says.

Tyrone sits up straight. His smile goes. 'Gloria,' he says. His voice is low and serious. Haider and Suzanne look round. 'You never pushed a man,' he says.

Gloria don't speak.

'You're saying this card is for the man?' Tyrone says.

Gloria nods.

'The police were talking shit. Sorry,' Tyrone says. His face is funny. She's not seen it look like that ever before.

Everything is dragged down. His mouth is a little bit open. 'The police know it's rubbish,' he says. 'They dropped the charges. No one thinks you done it. It's finished. No one's gonna ask you questions about it again.'

He touches her hand. She's standing in front of him, looking down at him. The sofa is soft and he is sinking back into it, he can't sit up straight.

He sighs. He rubs his lips with his hand.

'Gloria, I'll give him the card, okay? I'll give him the card. But don't talk about it again. It's over. Just forget about it, okay? The man's okay, and you never did nothing, and just forget about it. Alright?'

2019

It's bright. Air smells like summertime, of hot rubbish and distant barbecues.

Gloria is walking when she sees him.

It's real this time. Her chest feels tight and heavy but the day stays the same. The sun is in the sky, a car shushes past, the daylight blinks when a plane goes over.

It's Jack.

He's right there. Outside the library, standing talking to two men Gloria don't know. He looks different. His hair is grown longer, brown with grey bits in. His skin is tanned.

Gloria stops walking. She don't want to hurt him. She hurt him before when it weren't him. She puts her hands in her pockets to stop herself. Her hands are wet with sweat. She don't want to hurt him but she don't want to go with him either. She don't want to go to his house and drink Coke and eat chips and listen to him talk about things breaking. Sit in that hot tight room with him.

A police car goes past, floating slowly through the afternoon. Jack hunches and turns away.

Gloria stays still. One of her feet is forward on the

purple-red pavement, ready to walk. She leans forward but she don't move. She's watching him. He looks around and sees her.

She feels things move around inside her. Everything tightens up. Every bit of her moves up, makes her face hot, leaves her belly cold and hard. Her eyes soft and open. Tears on her cheeks.

Jack raises his eyebrows. Lines come on his forehead. His face is looser, skin pulling down beside his mouth. His lips are thin. It's him. She knows him.

He smiles a tiny bit. His eyes are very blue and they shine like they're wet.

Gloria shifts her weight onto the foot that's in front and starts to walk. She has to go past him. She gets closer, seeing all of his face, the dots of his pores, his hair curling over the tops of his ears, the dry sound of him breathing, a hand disappearing into his grey pocket, little gold hairs on his arm. Blue-green ink.

His hand moves.

Gloria stops. She steps back.

But he ain't reaching for her. There's a blue tobacco pouch and a little white paper. Stained fingers. Black dirt in the nails.

She don't look away. His eyes stare at her. He nods, jerking his head towards where she's going.

'Go on,' he says.

She looks at him.

'Go on,' he says again. He puts his hands out, holding

them back and away from his body, away from her. To show he won't touch her. The paper and the tobacco pouch pinched in one palm.

She walks. One step, then the next, until she is past him. Just past him. She turns and looks. He is watching her. He opens his mouth like he's about to say something.

Gloria turns away. She keeps walking.

Jack don't call out to her. He don't say Gloria. He lets her go. She hears him talking to the men. His voice is hot and floats away behind her. She can't hear words, just the sound of his voice. She knows it. Something stuck in his throat. He coughs, wet and rough. She keeps walking. His voice stays behind her. She don't know what he's saying and her ears stop trying to hear it. There's cars and sirens and her own feet on the pavement, her own breathing loud and jagged. It hurts in her chest.

She walks and walks. Her breath is coming fast. The day looks all fizzy, twinkling on and off. She used to walk down this street when she was a kid to go to the library and there's dog mess on the street and Mum grabs her hand and pulls her so she don't tread in it. Jack is all the way behind her and he ain't followed her. He don't grab her arm. She sees a flash of herself in the window of a parked car, a woman walking. She walks round down all these streets she been walking on forever, past the corner shop with blue writing on the sign. There are girls playing on the corner, learning a dance.

On the big road with the buses. She goes to the lights and crosses. She goes into the park. She's shaking a bit and her mouth feels dry. There are different sounds in here, the traffic noise is quieter, the car horns and the engines and sirens are faded, but the people noise is more, boys shouting, kids shouting, voices talking. Sunshine is all over her. Hot on her skin. She looks up at the leaves flickering against the sunlight. Shifting like the sea. The air starts coming in more. She walks on the path. Kids on the swings ticking backwards and forwards. There is words sprayed on the path in bright pink spray paint. She don't know what it says. She treads on it, her shoe covering the bright pink. There is people on all the benches and nowhere she can sit. She walks. Her legs are tired.

Near the fountain she finds a free bench. She sits down. Sweat comes on her skin. A man walks past with a small dog on a lead. The dog looks like it's smiling. A big dog comes past and the small dog barks and jumps at it. The big dog flinches away. The man pulls the little dog, its collar straining round its neck. Over near the fountain there are people walking in the flower beds, holding sticks to pick up rubbish with. They are laughing and talking to each other. A man holds a bin bag that glows light brown in the sunshine. A woman is inside the little fence around the fountain. She uses her stick to pull muddy pieces of rubbish out of the green water in the fountain. Water drips from her stick. The fountain is covered in bright-green weeds. Where's the sharps bin, someone calls. The woman puts dripping rubbish in her bag. She points. Over next to Jay. Be careful don't touch it. She stretches, leaning side to side. She drops her stick and her bin bag over the fence and starts to climb over. She gets stuck part way, a leg on either side of the fence. 'Help me,' she yells, and a woman comes and holds her hand and she gets over back onto the path. She's laughing. She leans on the woman and holds her arm. She says something to her. Then she turns around and walks towards Gloria's bench. She comes over and sits down, the other end from Gloria. There's mud on her jeans. She sighs and leans back. Her face is red from the sun. She tips her head back and smiles to herself. Gloria likes the way she looks. Busy and happy.

'Hello,' Gloria says.

The woman looks at her.

'Hello,' the woman says. Her eyes are light blue. She lifts her hips up so she can reach in her pocket. She pulls out a pack of cigarettes. 'Mind if I smoke?' she says.

Gloria shakes her head.

The woman puts a fag in her mouth and clicks the lighter. Orange fire. The dry hot smell of smoke. She takes a deep breath on her cigarette.

'Don't overdo it, will ya,' a man shouts at her. He's holding a bin bag.

The woman smiles. 'These lot are doing my head in,' she says to Gloria, but she don't sound angry. There's laughter in her voice. She nods towards the people clearing rubbish. 'Come and help us if you want,' she says. 'We're cleaning up the park a bit. Litter picking and that. There's cake.'

Gloria looks at the people around the fountain. A girl is picking up an old beer can with a stick. The can is shining on the end of the stick, bright silver. She puts it into a bin bag and it disappears.

'We got plenty of spare litter pickers,' the woman says. 'Up to you.'

'Okay,' says Gloria.

Okayo kayo kay. Sharp crack in the middle.

She plays it round. She likes it.

Acknowledgements

First and foremost, thank you to Neil Griffiths, a brilliant editor, for seeing the potential in this story and turning it into the book it is now. And to Damian Lanigan, for the same.

Thanks also to Sarah Terry, an excellent copy editor.

Thanks to Luke Bird for the perfect cover image.

Thanks to Stephen Meade and Daniel Langsman (aka Shanks & Bigfoot) for permission to quote lyrics from the song 'Sweet Like Chocolate'.

Fraser Massey, a true gent. Thank you for all the drinks we shared, the long discussions, for reading an early draft of this novel and giving excellent feedback, and for your generosity and friendship. I wish you could have seen this book make its appearance. You are sorely missed.

Ally Wilkes, thanks for the advice on court proceedings (any mistakes are mine). And for all the venting and cat pics.

Mo – thank you for your generous advice.

Bronwyn Jones, Apala Chowdhury, Kate Fitzpatrick, Richard Stirling, Rebecca Wright, Danielle Rosenstein – you were all kind enough to read an early draft of this novel. Thank you for your comments and support.

Abir Mukherjee, thanks for your encouragement when you read an early sample of this novel.

This book is dedicated to Benjamin Zephaniah. Thank you for your friendship, for the vegan solidarity, and for encouraging my writing.

Peter Apps, my first reader on this and so much else. Thank you for your faith in me and your steadfast belief in my writing. Thanks for getting it. And for your insightful feedback and advice.

Mum and Dad, I am grateful for more than I can say and owe you more than I probably realise. Thank you both for your love and support, and for the many hours I spent writing this novel under your roof.

Deb Canning, thank you for always backing me in taking a less conventional path.

Craig Dyer – thank you for your love, your faith in me, and for the space and time. I love you.

GLORIA DON'T SPEAK

LUCY APPS

First published in 2025
by Weatherglass Books

Copyright © 2025 Lucy Apps

All rights reserved. No part of this publication may be reproduced or transmitted in any form or by any means, electronic or mechanical, including photocopy, recording or any information storage and retrieval system, without permission in writing from the publisher.

This book is a work of fiction. Names, characters, businesses, organizations, places and events are either the product of the author's imagination or used fictitiously. Any resemblance to actual persons, living or dead, or events is entirely coincidental.

A CIP record for this book is published by the British Library

ISBN: 978-1-0687941-7-9

Cover design: Luke Bird
Typesetting: James Tookey

Printed in the U.K. by CPI Books
www.weatherglassbooks.com

Weatherglass
Books